To Raquel,
Enjoy this great adventure!
Harvey

The Adventures of Charlie Pierce

The Barefoot Mailman

by Harvey E. Oyer III

Illustrations by James Balkovek

Map Illustration by Jeanne Brady

www.TheAdventuresofCharliePierce.com

Become a friend of Charlie Pierce on Facebook

All rights reserved. No part of this book may be reproduced or transmitted in any form or by any means, electronic or mechanical, including photocopying, recording, or by any information storage and retrieval system, without written permission from the author, except for the inclusion of brief quotations in a review.

ISBN 978-0-9964086-5-3

Copyright © 2015 by Harvey E. Oyer III

Published by:
Middle River Press
Oakland Park, Florida
middleriverpress.com.
info@middleriverpress.com

Printed in the U.S.A.
Second printing

Dedication

To my beautiful daughter, Eve. You are the greatest blessing of my life.

Acknowledgments

I wish to acknowledge the dedicated, outstanding work of editor Jon VanZile, illustrator James Balkovek, MFA, map illustrator Jeanne Brady, and the folks at Middle River Press. I also want to acknowledge the writings of Charles W. Pierce and Lillie Pierce Voss, from which I take many of these stories.

Introduction

This is the fourth book in a series of books about the adventures of young Charlie Pierce, one of South Florida's earliest pioneer settlers. The story follows teenage Charlie and his fearless little sister, Lillie, in the late 1800s, when South Florida was America's last frontier. Together with his Seminole friend, Tiger, Charlie experienced one of the most intriguing and exotic lives imaginable. His adventures as a young boy growing up in the wild, untamed jungles of Florida became legendary. Perhaps no other person experienced firsthand as many important events and met as many influential characters in South Florida's history.

For more information about the Pierce family's adventures, go to
www.TheAdventuresofCharliePierce.com
Become a friend of Charlie Pierce on **Facebook**
Facebook.com/CharliePierceBooks

Table of Contents

One: **Snakebite!** 11
Two: **The Sugar Mill** 19
Three: **A Reluctant Pledge** 27
Four: **The Coconut Hunter** 35
Five: **Lillie the Tagalong** 41
Six: **The Orange Grove House of Refuge** 47
Seven: **Nagging Doubt** 57
Eight: **The Ominous Inlet** 63
Nine: **The New River House of Refuge** 73
Ten: **Our First Fizzies** 81
Eleven: **Trouble Shows Up** 91
Twelve: **An Apology** 101
Thirteen: **Bandit's Secret** 107
Fourteen: **Lillie's Sprint** 115
Fifteen: **A Papa's Wisdom** 121
Sixteen: **The Most Expensive Bathtub** 129
Seventeen: **The Barefoot Mailman** 137
Who Were the Barefoot Mailmen? 143
Who was William H. Gleason? 147
About Charlie Pierce 151
About the Author 155

Chapter One

Snakebite!

"Rattlesnake!"

I froze in mid-swing, my long-handled hoe hanging above my head. The last thing I wanted to do was get bit by a rattlesnake out in the middle of our sugarcane field.

Then I heard the flat boom of a shotgun echo across the island. It came from the direction of the house.

I dropped the hoe and took off at a dead sprint through the half-acre plot of sugarcane. It was summer, and the cane was almost a full year old, so the plants were taller than me. Their long, rough leaves scraped at my face and arms as I ran through the rows.

When I burst into the open field at the edge of the cane plot, I saw in an instant what had happened. Papa was down on the ground, already tearing away his pant leg, and I could see he'd been bit. Two bright drops of blood ran down his ankle. Nearby, Uncle Will stood over the body of a five-foot diamondback rattler that he had just about blown in half with the smoking shotgun still in his hands.

"Papa!" I said, skidding to a stop. "How bad is it?"

He looked up, gritting his teeth from under his hat of woven palm fronds. "I wasn't watching, and that darn snake was sunning himself. I didn't see him until I almost stepped on him. Happened so fast I couldn't jump back in time."

"What should I do?" I asked, trying not to sound as scared as I was. We lived on Hypoluxo Island, so a trip to get Doc Potter meant taking a boat all the way up the lake, then hiking along paths through thick jungle and hoping the doctor was even at home. Even running, it would take a few hours to get help, and that might be too long. A big snake like this one could easily kill even a full-size man like Papa if left untreated. If it had been Lillie or me… I shuddered.

"You run and go get help," Uncle Will said, tearing his eyes away from the snake. "I'll see about getting some of that venom out."

His short blade was already in his hand. I knew what he meant to do: He was going to make a small cut where the snake had bit Papa and try to squeeze out the venom before it could travel much farther up his leg and reach Papa's heart. The skin on Papa's ankle was

already turning red and swelling up around the puncture marks. The venom was acting quickly.

"Hurry up, Charlie!" Papa said, his face white. It was the first time in my life I'd seen Papa looking scared. "Go ahead," Papa said to Uncle Will. "Make it fast."

I was just turning to run for the dock when Lillie suddenly appeared running down the path toward us from the house. "Wait!" she yelled. "Uncle Will! Wait!"

Uncle Will held back. It was a serious matter to make a cut out here in the jungle. An infection could be just as deadly as the snakebite itself.

"Don't cut him!" Lillie said. "There's another way to treat it."

Uncle Will and Papa exchanged a glance, and I could see they weren't sure. Even waiting a few minutes could mean the venom might reach Papa's heart.

"Please!" Lillie said. "I know what to do! Just let me get something!"

Papa reached a decision and nodded. Uncle Will slipped his knife away and squatted next to Papa. "You just stay still," Uncle Will said quietly. "You'll get your heart pumping and send that venom up your leg faster. I sure hope Lillie knows what she's doing."

I watched Lillie run back toward the house and sent a little prayer with her. I was every bit as confused as Papa and Uncle Will about Lillie's plan, but that was the thing about Lillie. She might be my little sister, but the way I figured it, if anyone on our island could fix a snake bite, it would be Lillie. Since we'd gotten back from our last adventure into the great Pa-Hay-Okee swamp, Lillie had taken up a new hobby: collecting dead rattlesnakes and tanning their skin. She even sold their rattles as baby rattles. Mama naturally hated Lillie's new hobby. "It's just not proper for a young lady to go scavenging around looking for dead snakes," she'd say. "Sometimes I wonder if the heat down here hasn't addled your brain, Lillie."

But Mama didn't really mean it. For the first time I could remember, Mama was actually happy about Lillie's schooling. The truth was, Lillie finally had found a subject that interested her: science. After spending time in the swamp with Jonathan Bartley and Professor Livingston from Yale University and learning how to identify plants and animals by their Latin names, Lillie had started reading every book she could on how to identify, classify, and preserve plants and animals. When she wasn't reading, she was picking people's brains on everything from why mosquitoes bite people to how the tides worked. Mama was tickled pink to see Lillie take an interest in learning, so she put up with the dead snakes.

"What do you think she's up to?" Uncle Will

said almost under his breath after Lillie had been gone for a few minutes.

"Don't know," Papa said. "But whatever she's doing, she better do it quick." He couldn't take his eyes off the red marks slowly traveling up his leg.

Finally, Lillie came running back across the field with a big pail of water and a brown glass bottle. When she unscrewed the cap, a familiar, eye-watering stink came out: turpentine. I knew turpentine was good for cleaning paintbrushes and washing sap stains out of my pants after I'd been climbing trees, but I had no idea what use turpentine would be in our present situation.

"Lillie girl," Papa said through gritted teeth. "What are you up to?"

"Turpentine?" Uncle Will added. "What on earth do you want with turpentine?"

Lillie made an exasperated face that looked like it had come straight from Mama. "I learned about this from the Seminoles, Papa. They use turpentine to draw the poison out. It works. Gray Cloud got bit by a snake last summer and it fixed him. Now give me your foot."

When he held his foot out, the bite looked worse than ever. It had been red just a minute before, but now it looked purple around the fang marks. I could see where the venom was leaving behind angry red lines as it traveled slowly up Papa's calf.

Lillie's face went pale.

"Lillie, you sure you don't want me to go get the doctor?" I asked.

She looked up at me, and I could see she was more nervous than she was letting on. "No, Charlie. You know…"

She let the words trail off, but I could guess what she was thinking: *There wouldn't be time anyway.*

By now, Papa's face was shiny with sweat, and his skin had gone a slight shade of gray.

Lillie's hand shook a little bit as she carefully poured a few tablespoons of turpentine into the pail of water, then helped Papa lower his foot into the potion. As his foot touched the stinky water, the sweat stood out on his forehead in fat drops. After his foot was fully submerged, he said in a hoarse voice, "If this venom doesn't get me, the turpentine just might."

"Hush," Lillie said.

"So now what?" Uncle Will put in. "How do you know it's working?"

"Now we wait," Lillie said. "And we'll know it's working when he can walk under his own power back to the house and into bed."

"Bed?!" Papa said. "I can't go to bed in the middle of the day! We got too much work to do out here."

Lillie gave Papa a look of reproach. "If this works, you're not going to be working for a while," she said. "Not by a long shot."

Uncle Will and Papa groaned. Aside from actually getting killed by a snake, getting laid up in bed was just about the worst thing that could happen. It was the rainy season in South Florida, and that meant everything was growing in double-time. There were pineapples to harvest from the field I'd planted last year and land to keep clear, wild trees to cut back, and vines to hack away with the big machete. Worse yet, the cane mill wasn't even half done, and we were on schedule to harvest the new sugarcane in just a few weeks. All summer long, I'd dreamed about the pure sugar we'd cook down from that cane juice once we got the cane mill finished. But now, with Papa grimacing in pain and a fresh-killed rattlesnake lying nearby in the sun, I would have given all the sugar in the world for Lillie's strange Seminole cure to work.

Chapter Two

The Sugar Mill

After we helped him inside, Papa lay in bed all afternoon, sweating and gasping for air. Mama hovered over him, dabbing away the sweat with a cloth she soaked in cool water, while Uncle Will paced around the cabin like a caged panther. I should have been outside working—I knew that Papa wouldn't want the work to stop—but I couldn't leave until I was sure he was alright.

The next morning, the worst had passed, but Papa complained that his leg burned like it was on fire, and his skin still smelled like turpentine. Worse yet, his ankle had swelled up like a puffer fish, and he had to lean on either me or Uncle Will if he wanted to walk anywhere.

Still, Papa couldn't bear lying in bed while there was work to be done, so he stationed himself in a chair on the porch with his big palm-frond hat covering his face, his swollen ankle propped up on a crate, and Mama fussing over him every time he tried to put his foot down and stand up. "You stay right there!"

she'd order. "At least until your foot looks human again."

He spent those next few days watching me and Uncle Will working on the cane mill, yelling out advice. It was hard work, and I didn't think we'd ever get the mill done before the first sugarcane crop was ready to harvest. Fortunately, once word of Papa's snake bite got around, a neighbor named Will Lanehart showed up to help us. Mr. Lanehart was a big carpenter with curly hair and scars on his hands from a lifetime of hard work. He was as strong as a black bear and he knew almost as much as Papa about farming in the sandy soil.

Better yet, Mr. Lanehart was full of good ideas when it came to the cane mill, and Papa often asked for Mr. Lanehart's opinion. The whole idea of sugarcane farming had come to Papa the year before, when he was looking for new crops in case the pineapples or some other crop failed. Papa had heard they grew sugarcane down in the West Indies on huge plantations and figured we could try our hand at it. If the sugarcane experiment worked, Papa said it would be just like growing gold. Pure sugar was in high demand everywhere from Key West to New York.

The problem was that it wasn't so easy to go from deciding to grow sugarcane to actually getting sugar. We had planted the sugarcane the summer before, burying long stalks horizontally just under the soil. It didn't take long before little sugarcane plants popped up through the soil. We watered the young plants, fed them with manure, and weeded the rows all year.

In the meantime, we had to build a cane mill to process the stalks into sugar after we harvested them. A cane mill was a simple enough contraption but not easy to build. It was made with big rollers that would crush the fresh-cut cane stalks and squeeze out the sweet juice. Once we had enough juice, we'd boil it down until all that was left was pure cane syrup and brown crystal sugar.

At least, this is how it was supposed to work. Not only had we never built or even seen a cane mill, but we also had no idea where to get a pot nearly big enough to boil down a decent batch of sugar. Mama's biggest pot was only big enough for a Sunday rooster, and there was no way she'd let us use it to boil cane juice. Uncle Will had put the word out that we were looking for a big kettle anywhere within sailing distance, but none had turned up so far.

Mr. Lanehart couldn't help with the kettle, but he did figure out how to solve the problem of making rollers to crush the cane stalks. A good cane mill needed really heavy and perfectly round logs for rollers, so the morning after he arrived, he set out into the woods and found some fine old mahogany trees. We cut them down and dragged the trunks to our property. With Papa watching from the porch, Mr. Lanehart next figured out a clever way to whittle these heavy logs into round rollers.

He drilled a handle into the end of each big log and used that to turn the log. Meanwhile, Uncle Will and I used sharp hand axes to whittle the log into a perfect cylinder, or at least mostly perfect.

"Watch out for that knot there!" Papa would call from the porch as we whittled away. "You don't want to knick that blade. Make sure it's straight now." When we weren't turning logs, there was still the whole farm to worry about, and even Lillie pitched in with regular farm work. The pineapple plants needed trimming by pulling off their old dead leaves and trying not to stab ourselves on their sharp spines. And of course there was all of our regular food crops, animals, and the million daily chores. Without Papa handling most of the workload, it suddenly felt like the farm had quadrupled in size.

It didn't help much that the regular summer rains had started. Every day, we'd wake up to the sun shining like a white-hot disc in the sky and work through the morning hours, dripping sweat and drinking water by the bucket. Then in the late afternoon, regular as clockwork, the big black clouds would build up to the west and come sweeping over us, trailing gray curtains of rain. We'd run inside during the rain to eat. After the rain ended, we'd head right back out, sloshing through the mud and sweating.

It was on just such an afternoon—with Uncle Will and me bent over a mahogany log while Mr. Lanehart turned the handle—that

we heard Lillie calling out. "A boat!" she cried. "Coming to dock!"

We exchanged a sweaty look over the log, set our tools down and headed for the dock.

"Who is it, Lillie?" Papa called out from the porch. He was still not walking on his foot.

"It's Hamilton!" she yelled over her shoulder, already running toward the dock.

I tried not to be annoyed at Lillie, but I couldn't help it. Hamilton had moved to our area the year before from Kentucky. He had a wild mop of blond hair, very blue eyes, and a thick accent. Everybody liked Hamilton, and I certainly didn't have anything against him. We'd helped him thatch his roof when he first set up his cottage on the west side of the lake. But he also had this strange effect on Lillie: She batted her eyes at him all the time and always showed off around him. It was irksome.

The four of us—me, Uncle Will, Lillie, and Mr. Lanehart—gathered on the dock and watched as he rowed the final yards toward us.

"Ahoy!" Hamilton called, bending his back to the oars. "I didn't expect a welcome party!"

Lillie actually giggled, and I wondered who had replaced my sister with this giddy new girl.

"Afternoon," Uncle Will called, helping Hamilton tie up. "We were just looking to take a break."

I saw right away that Hamilton didn't look so good. He had black bags under his normally bright eyes, and his nose was red and chapped. He rose to his feet slowly, coughed into his hand, and climbed from the boat. As he did, he leaned over and grabbed a thick leather pouch from the boat's floor.

My eyes widened when I realized what he was carrying. Written on the side of the pouch in big white letters were the words, "U.S. Mail." I noticed Uncle Will and Mr. Lanehart also staring at the pouch, and I could only imagine how excited Mama would be. She was always waiting to get news from her Chicago relatives and read the ladies magazines from New York City.

Mail was a rarity in our part of Florida. I was old enough to remember when it only came once a month, sometimes even less. It had only been coming weekly for the last year or so, after Mr. Bradley got the mail contract.

"You've got the mail?" Lillie exclaimed, sounding like Santa Claus himself had just landed on our island.

"Sure do," Hamilton said, swinging the bag over his shoulder and wiping sweat from his forehead. "Guess who got the new contract to deliver mail? From now on, I guess I'll be your personal mailman."

I swear I saw Lillie blush.

"I thought Mr. Bradley had the mail route?"

Uncle Will said, walking next to Hamilton as we headed up toward our house.

"Not anymore, sir," Hamilton said. "He got tired of it, and Guy and Louis were sick of walking the pouch for him, so I'm taking it over."

"You alright, son?" Mr. Lanehart asked, staring closely at Hamilton. "You look like death got warmed over and served up for breakfast."

"Yessir," he said in a tired voice. "Just got a cold, I suppose."

I heard Mama calling and saw her standing on the front porch, waving at Hamilton. As we got closer, she offered him lemonade. "And you'll be staying for dinner, of course?" she asked.

Hamilton grinned weakly. "Mrs. Pierce, I wouldn't miss one of your dinners for all the tea in China."

Chapter Three

A Reluctant Pledge

"I don't much like the sound of it," Papa said, frowning.

Mr. Lanehart had left before dinner, so the rest of us were gathered around the table. The remains of Mama's excellent meal were still on the table, and Hamilton's precious mail pouch rested next to him. He hadn't let it out of his sight since landing on our island.

"Well, I do understand your concern," Hamilton said to Papa, looking more tired and sicker then ever. "It's not that I'm arguing with you, Mr. Pierce, but the fact is, Gleason's actually the man who has the contract with the U.S. Postal Service. So if you want to deliver the mail in southern Florida, he's the man you're going to work for."

Papa's frown grew even deeper. I understood why. Not too long ago, William H. Gleason had tried to force us off Hypoluxo Island and take our land. Only my plume-hunting trip into Pa-Hay-Okee with Tiger Bowlegs and my

friends, Guy and Louis Bradley, had saved the island. After I came back, I gave the money to Mama and Papa to save the island from Mr. Gleason and vowed to never again hunt for plume birds.

Ever since, the name Gleason had been like a curse word around our house.

We weren't the only people who didn't like Gleason. Papa said he was the worst kind of carpetbagger, and I'd heard all sorts of stories about his shady dealings. During the War Between the States, he'd opened banks all over the country for various reasons and gotten involved in all kinds of land deals. When he came down to Florida after the war, he had plans to get rich buying up land and turning it into farms—and according to Papa, he didn't care how he did it. He tried to get politicians to write laws just for him, came up with wild schemes to drain swamps and dig canals, and managed to get himself elected to five offices at the same time.

At one point, he even tried to have the rightful governor of Florida, Harrison Reed, impeached and declared himself the governor while the legislature was out of session. When the local sheriff wouldn't let him into the state capitol building, Gleason set up in a nearby hotel and signed documents as "Governor William H. Gleason." He only lasted a month before the Florida Supreme Court declared that Reed was the actual governor, and Gleason was removed from office.

"How'd a man like that manage to get the mail contract anyway?" Papa said glumly.

Hamilton shrugged. "Don't know for sure. You know he's connected up in Washington. But the point isn't that I'd be working for him. You know we need regular mail here, especially if this place opens up to the railroad. I'm happy to be the one who delivers it. Besides, I really need the job. Farming ain't as easy here as they cracked it up to be."

Mama leaned forward. "Is it true then what they're saying? That a wealthy industrialist is thinking about bringing a railroad to South Florida?"

"Yes, ma'am," Hamilton said. "I know for certain it is true. His name is Henry Flagler. He made it big in Standard Oil and now owns hotels up in St. Augustine. It's a fact that he's already got most of land he needs to lay rail all the way down to Miami. Once that happens, Florida will never be the same again. It'll be real progress."

Hamilton dropped his voice to a hoarse whisper. "But I'll tell you something secret. He doesn't have *all* the land he needs, not quite yet. This pouch here," he said, nudging the mail pouch with his foot, "it's got a big envelope from Tallahassee for the boys down in Miami. I think it's the official state map of where Flagler plans on running that railway and which pieces of property he still needs. From what I hear, there are just a few pieces of property left. Until he gets those last pieces of property, he can't build his railroad."

Papa grunted. "That sounds like a mighty big *until*. Any landowner who finds out Flagler wants their land for a railroad will ask for the moon."

Hamilton shrugged. "Maybe, but maybe not. Who wouldn't want the rail to come here? It would mean jobs, a better life for everyone. Only a real crook would try to blackmail Flagler like that."

"A crook like Gleason," Papa grumbled. "You better watch yourself, or he'll try to steal those plans from you."

"I don't think even he'd stoop that low," Hamilton said. "He might have the contract, but the mail is a federal matter. Anyone who tampers with it can end up in jail, even Mr. Gleason."

"And you don't think he'd just try to take it?" Papa said.

Hamilton frowned, but it dissolved into a round of coughing. "Well, no, I guess I don't. What kind of man would steal from his own employee?"

"Gleason would," Papa said without hesitation.

"Come now," Mama said to Papa. "There's no call to badger our guest any more about it.

Goodness, you'd think he'd done something wrong by the way you're acting."

Papa grunted, but he leaned back and didn't say anything else.

Hamilton sighed. "I hope you understand, Mr. Pierce. Like I said, Mr. Gleason might hold the contract, but when it comes to walking this mail pouch from here to Miami and back, you can believe I'm as true and honest as they come."

"I know you are," Papa said. "It's just I haven't forgotten what Gleason tried to do to us…and I guess I'm not sure I like the thought of a railroad chugging through the woods down here, bringing down cars full of people. I know you can't hold back progress, but I guess that doesn't stop a man from wishing."

Hamilton nodded. "I understand. And actually… well, it's not really an accident I stopped by here. I was hoping to ask a favor, but now I'm not so sure…"

When he didn't go on, Mama said, "Don't worry about my husband, Mr. Hamilton. Go ahead and ask, and we'll help if we can."

"Well, if I'm going to keep this job, I need someone to second the contract. In case I get sick so bad I can't walk or can't do the route, my second would take it over." He looked at Papa, then down at Papa's foot. "I was hoping I might be able to talk you into it, but…"

Papa looked down at his bandaged foot and grimaced, then he laughed a little bit. "Well, obviously I can't be walking the mail on this foot right now. But even after it gets better, I can't really take on that kind of commitment. I've got this farm to keep up, and no offense to you, Hamilton, I could never work for a man who tried to run my family off our land."

Hamilton's face fell, and everybody was silent for a few minutes. Then a flush crept into my face as Hamilton looked over at me hopefully.

"What about you, Charlie? You're old enough to make the trip, and it's not likely you'd ever have to. It would only be if I was laid up sick or got hurt, and I'm doing my best to make sure neither of those happen. And if you ever did have to, I'd pay you for it. It's good money. The route's worth $600 a year."

"Um, well…" I stalled. The truth was, I always did like the chance to make some extra money. But I'd heard from Guy and Louis that the mail route was hard work. They hated doing it when their father couldn't make the trip. It was a three-day walk down the beach to Miami, then three days back, pushing against the bugs, rain, and wind the whole time. After you got back, you'd get one day of rest, then another pouch would arrive, and you'd have to start it all over again.

Then again, I thought of Mr. Lanehart taking time away from his own land and family to come help us after Papa was bit by the snake.

Neighbors needed to stick together down here in the Florida jungle, and Hamilton was a good friend and neighbor. "Yeah," I said reluctantly, "I guess I could second the contract."

Hamilton's face lit up with a tired smile, but Papa cut across him and said, "Now, Charlie, you're sure about this? You know it's a serious commitment you're making?"

"Yes, Papa," I said. "I know, but if he needs a second or he'll lose the job…well, I'd want someone to do the same for me. You don't have any problem with me doing it, do you?"

"No, I don't, Charlie," Papa said. "I just want to make sure you mean it."

I nodded slowly while Hamilton eagerly shook my hand. He reached into his pouch and produced a three-page contract. "Thanks, Charlie! Like I said, I don't ever plan on needing you, but if you could just sign on the dotted line here, that'll make it official."

I took up a pen and hoped I wasn't making a mistake as I carefully made my signature on the final page of the contract.

Chapter Four

The Coconut Hunter

The next morning, I woke up to find Papa hobbling around the house with a stout cane. "Morning, Charlie." he said, glancing at me. "Now that Mr. Lanehart is gone, I can't just sit around all day, no matter what your Mama says."

"You sure you can work like that?" I asked.

"I'm sure I can figure something out."

In the minute of silence that followed, we heard Hamilton coughing in the next room, where he had slept last night. I was just about to go check on him when I heard voices from the front yard and looked outside to see Mr. Lanehart talking to Uncle Will. Then Mama bustled in with Lillie tagging along behind her.

"My goodness, it's like a carnival around here this morning," she said, glancing out the window. "I wonder if Mr. Lanehart will stay for breakfast?"

But when Uncle Will came back in alone, he announced that Mr. Lanehart had only dropped by for a minute to tell us that he'd heard about a large iron kettle for sale down at the Hunt place on Biscayne Bay.

"So," Uncle Will said, "I guess I'll be heading down that way as soon as I can get the boat ready. He says the kettle's a big one they salvaged from a wrecked ship a few months back. Supposed to be in pretty good shape."

Hamilton appeared in the doorway, looking paler and sicker than ever. "Morning," he said through a stuffy nose.

"Oh my, Mr. Hamilton," Mama said. "You look like you need to crawl right back into bed!"

"Can't, ma'am," he said glumly. "The mail doesn't care if I'm sick."

I tried to make myself invisible, hoping it wouldn't occur to him to ask me to deliver the mail pouch. The last thing I wanted to do this week was walk the six days to Miami and back.

"Hey," Uncle Will said to Hamilton, "you should come down with me. Turns out I have to sail down to Biscayne Bay. I'd be happy to drop you in Miami at the same time. Save you the long walk and give you some time to rest up."

Hamilton looked relieved and said, "When you a'leaving?"

"Just as soon as I can get the *Magellan*

rigged, probably a couple of days," Uncle Will said.

Hamilton looked like he was seriously considering it but then shook his head. "Sorry, unless you're leaving today, I can't wait that long. I can't be late with the mail, especially my first week on the job."

"Suit yourself." Uncle Will shrugged and headed out for his house on the north end of the island to get the *Magellan* ready to make the trip.

It ended up being a gloomy breakfast, with Papa muttering to himself and Hamilton looking like he might fall over at any moment. Mama was obviously worried about him, especially as we watched him start to shoulder his gear and heavy canteens full of water. I didn't think he was going to make it to the door, but before I could offer to help, Lillie jumped up and said, "Mr. Hamilton, you can't go like that! Put down those heavy water jugs and follow me."

I tried not to roll my eyes at the prospect of Lillie giving orders to a nearly grown man like Hamilton, but stopped in surprise when he did just what she said.

"C'mon," she said. "I'll show you a trick so you at least don't have to carry twenty pounds of water on your back all the way to Miami."

Hamilton looked grateful. "Anything that'll help, I'll take it," he said.

So right after breakfast, I was treated to the spectacle of Lillie leading a very pale Hamilton outside to the coconut grove. I watched out the window as he stood under one of the trees and watched her scamper up to harvest a green coconut. Her climbing method made her look just like a South Sea Islander. First, she took a short piece of rope and looped it around the trunk, then jumped up and grabbed the trunk with both bare feet. She climbed the tall trunk in a series of jerking motions, jumping up the tree like a grasshopper. When she got to the top, she yanked down a few coconuts that fell to the ground with thuds. When she was done, she slid back down the tree, hacked the tops off, and handed one of the nuts to Hamilton to drink. He looked inside before tilting it up and letting the rich coconut juice run down his chin.

When it came his turn to try, I saw how hard Lillie's method really was. Hamilton scarcely made it five feet up the trunk before sliding back down.

"Mama," I said, "you sure Lillie should be teaching him how to climb trees today? It looks like he can barely walk."

"Well, I'm sure if he couldn't handle it, he'd just tell her," Mama said distractedly from the tub where she was washing dishes. I let the matter drop.

Later, when I came back in, Lillie was smiling ear to ear. I soon found out why. Hamilton had agreed to let Lillie sail him down the lake to the haulover so he could be on his

way south to start the mail route. Lillie seemed to want any excuse at all to spend time with Hamilton.

In no time, we were waving good-bye to Hamilton as he and Lillie shoved off and turned south, heading down the lake. I was a little worried about him—he looked too sick to make that long walk alone—but he insisted on going. At least Lillie was saving him a mile of walking by sailing him down the lake.

And I knew he was right about one other thing: There was no stopping the mail.

Chapter Five

Lillie the Tagalong

With just me and Papa left at home, there was no way we could do the heavy work of making rollers from mahogany logs. Instead, I spent that morning on our roof, pulling out rotted thatch and weaving in new green palmetto fronds.

Like almost every house in South Florida, we used the Seminole technique of making our roofs from palmetto fronds that we wove together into a tight covering. It made a watertight roof and didn't cost any money—only time and effort. The only problem was that the fronds didn't last very long in the heat and rain. Every other year or so, we had to climb up on the roof to replace rotted fronds with fresh green ones.

It was a messy job. The old brown fronds fell apart when you tugged on them, and they were full of big palmetto bugs. If there was one thing I hated, it was the fat, brown palmetto bugs.

I was still working on the roof when Lillie

returned in the late morning, just as dark clouds were stacking up for another afternoon of summer storms. I was grateful for the break, even if the house felt empty after so many visitors. Papa was a bundle of frustrated energy and kept listing off all the things that weren't getting done until Mama told him to relax and that she was sure Lillie and I could handle the farm for a while until Uncle Will got back.

Finally, ten days after he had left, we saw Uncle Will's sail coming down the lake. Papa and I were working on the log rollers, making slow progress. Papa straightened up and waited with me at the dock for Uncle Will. I was anxious to see the new kettle. As he got nearer, I saw it sitting on the deck: a thick lump of iron that looked like a huge hollow cannonball. I could almost taste the sweet sugar we were going to cook up in it.

But even before Uncle Will docked, I could tell something was wrong.

"Hey, Will," Papa said. "That kettle's a fine looking one. What are you looking so glum about?"

Uncle Will shook his head, and for the next few minutes there was the confusion of docking and tying up lines. When he finally got on the dock, he said, "Hamilton didn't happen to get a late start, did he?"

"Why no," Papa said. "Lillie sailed him

down to the haulover the same morning you left for your house. That was about ten days ago."

Uncle Will frowned. "I was afraid you would say that."

"Why? What's wrong?"

"After I got the kettle from Hunt, I figured I'd head to the Brickell place for supplies. They saw me coming and thought maybe I was carrying the mail. I told 'em that Hamilton had the mail and he should have been there and gone already, but they said he never arrived in Miami…" His words trailed off. "I'm wondering if he was too sick to make that trip and he's holed up somewhere in the jungle suffering."

Now it was Papa's turn to frown. "I hope not. The wilderness is no place for a man as sick as he was."

The men looked at each other evenly, and I could see there were a lot of unspoken words. From heat and rattlesnakes to panthers, the jungle was full of danger.

"Papa?" I said. "You think something happened to Hamilton? We've got to do something, right? We can't leave him out there alone."

Papa looked at me and sighed. "No, we can't, Charlie. You know as well as anyone the dangers in these parts. A search party is going to have to be mounted." He paused. "I just…

Will, do you think you could go around the lake and round up some of the neighbors? I'm in no condition to go myself with my leg still bitten up like this, and what with taking a week off, I really can't afford the time. Maybe Lanehart and the Bradleys can pitch a hand and…" He shrugged.

I knew for a fact how hard it would be for any of the men to take time off during the rainy season. Farm work is always hard, but in the summer, with everything growing double-time and half of every day given over to rain, there's twice as much work in half the time. You could leave a field alone for a week and come back to find it overtaken with weeds and vines or eaten down to the sandy soil by big lubber grasshoppers.

"I'll go," I said suddenly. "I can leave right away and I know the way." Papa started to object, but I said, "I seconded the contract, Papa. It's my responsibility. I'll be home in a week at most. You know I'll be careful."

Papa seemed to consider it, then said the last thing in the world I expected him to say: "Okay, Charlie, but take Lillie with you."

"Lillie?!" I said. "But Mama will—"

Papa shook his head firmly. "I'll talk to your mother, Charlie. I'd feel better if you two were together. You know that girl can survive in the woods for months on her own, and she knows the land between here and

Miami as well as you do. You take Lillie, and hurry. I need you back here soon, and if Mr. Hamilton really is in trouble, he'll need you right away."

I nodded. "Okay," I said, wondering how it always happened that I managed to get stuck with my little sister whenever something exciting happened.

Chapter Six

The Orange Grove House of Refuge

We were ready to leave within the half-hour. We figured there was enough daylight left that we'd make the Orange Grove House of Refuge around nightfall, leaving us plenty of light to see any clues along the beach. Our plan was to spend the first night at the Orange Grove House of Refuge, the second night at the New River House of Refuge and the third night at the Brickell Trading Post in Miami, where Hamilton had failed to show up with the mail. We'd follow his exact route.

Like I'd predicted, Mama was worried about us going alone, but she also understood. If one of us had been lost in the jungle, she'd expect every neighbor for miles around to pitch in and help. It was also true that both of us knew this stretch of land like our own yard. Lillie had been born in the Orange Grove House of Refuge, and we had lived there when I was younger. We had made this walk so many times, both of us could probably do it with our eyes closed.

We packed light: a small sack of hard biscuits, some fishing line and hooks, and a small canteen for water. We did, however, pick up one surprise guest. Lillie's pet raccoon, Bandit, ran out after us as we headed for the boat.

"Lillie," I said. "Tell that varmint to go back to the woods. He can't come with us."

Lillie looked shocked. "What are you talking about?" she demanded. "Of course he's coming with us."

"That doesn't make any sense—"

"What doesn't make sense is leaving him behind. It's not like we'll have to feed him or anything."

I huffed a sigh. "Fine. Let's just get going then."

Uncle Will sailed us down the lake to the haulover. On the way down, I leaned against the warm metal of the kettle and watched the clear water rushing by. I was worried about Hamilton—it was a serious matter to get lost in the thicket of creeks, haulovers, hammocks, and inlets, especially for someone like Hamilton who was newer to the area—but something else was bothering me. It was a bad thought, one I sincerely hoped wasn't true: What if Hamilton had taken those secret plans to Gleason after all?

I couldn't believe he'd do a thing like that, but then he said he needed money, and I knew what it was like to need money. I'd gone plume bird hunting for money, and even though I'd seen with my own eyes the terrible things the hunters were doing to the birds, I'd still gone ahead with it anyway. What if Hamilton had made a decision like that?

I glanced at Lillie. She was sitting up on the bow with her legs dangling over the edge and playing with Bandit. I wanted to ask her opinion, mainly so she could convince me I was being suspicious and foolish, but something stopped me. For now at least, I figured it was a better idea just to keep my mouth shut and see what we found along the way.

It seemed like just a few minutes later that Lillie and I were waving good-bye to Uncle Will and scrambling up the beach dune through a thicket of sea grape and gumbo limbo trees. The beach and ocean came into view when we gained the top of the dune. Even with the clouds in the distance, it was a perfect summer afternoon. The ocean was a particular shade of green, and its surface was almost flat. Even from the top of the dune, we could see the flash and shadows of fish swimming in the shallow water and the little wading birds running along the shore.

"C'mon, Charlie," Lillie said, already sliding down the dune. "We better get moving. And let's keep our eyes open, just in case."

I knew what she meant, and we walked mostly in silence on the hard-packed sand where high tide had smoothed it out. Along one stretch of beach, we passed five or six small fish that had been bitten clean in half and washed up on shore.

"Barracuda, I bet," Lillie said, and I nodded.

We walked for a bit longer in silence, scanning the beach and dune for any sign of Hamilton but seeing nothing. There were no footprints in the sand, but I wasn't surprised. The tide would have washed away footprints down by the water days ago, and the wind and rain would have taken care of any tracks higher up the beach. Even the Seminoles would have trouble following tracks along the beach.

"What's got your tongue?" Lillie finally said, kicking idly at sand as she walked. "You've hardly said three words since we started."

It was on the tip on my tongue to say something about my worries over Hamilton and the maps. But I couldn't bring myself to accuse our friend of stealing plans from the state and giving them to a man like Gleason. I didn't even really believe it myself, and I silently cursed myself for being suspicious.

"Nothing," I said. "Just worried is all."

Lillie gave a sidelong look. "If you say so."

I was relieved when Lillie got distracted watching Bandit try to chase down minnows in the shallow pools between sandbars created by the outgoing tide. It was funny, I had to admit, watching him dash around and sneeze when salt water got into his nose.

***

We knew we were getting close when we spotted a break in the dunes and saw the house itself. The grove of wild orange trees that gave the house its name was on a flat part of land just down the beach a ways. The trees had finished their bloom and were covered with tiny oranges the size of my thumb. I had spent a lot of time in this grove when I was younger and knew the oranges wouldn't be ready for harvest until fall, and even then they were too sour to eat on their own. But Mama still liked them—she'd use them to marinate fish or venison.

After we passed over the dune, we walked through the field of palmetto surrounding the House of Refuge. The house was two stories, with a big wraparound porch and a heavy pitched roof.

"Charlie Pierce! Lillie!" a voice called out, and I saw Steve Andrews coming out of the front door, waving happily.

Andrews was the keeper of the house, a position Papa had held years ago when we lived there. The keeper had an important job: to keep the House of Refuge in good condition and stocked with all the supplies people would need in a crisis. That meant food, medicine, and fresh water. The House of Refuge was open to anyone who needed help along the shore, including shipwrecked sailors, lost travelers, and of course, the mailman as he made his way south toward Miami and back.

Mr. Andrews was a tall and lanky man with a large, thin nose that was as red and rawboned as his knuckles and hair. He was the only person from England I'd ever met, and I loved the way he talked.

"Hello!" I called out, and Lillie and I hurried toward him.

A woman emerged from the house, and I saw it was Annie, his wife. She had come from up North in Michigan and was the only grown-up we knew who insisted we call her by her first name. If I slipped up and called her "Mrs. Andrews," she'd always say, "Annie, dear. Mrs. Andrews is my mother-in-law." Annie and Mama were close friends. Whenever they saw each other, they talked about all the things up North they missed, like the opera and symphony. Personally, it didn't sound like we were missing much.

"So to what do we owe the pleasure of your visit?" Mr. Andrews said as we climbed the porch and shook hands hello. "I must admit you weren't the next people I expected to see on my doorstep."

"Actually," I said, "we're looking for Hamilton. He's got the mail route and left our place for here ten days ago. Have you seen him?"

"Why yes," Annie said. "He was here. Sick, the poor thing. And," she hesitated, "truth is, we expected to see him back here ourselves on the return trip, but he never came back. Has something happened?"

"We don't know," I said. "Only that he never showed up at the Brickell place in Miami like he was supposed to either."

Annie and Mr. Andrews shared a worried look. "Like the missus says, he was terribly sick," Mr. Andrews said. "He had dinner with us, then left the next day, even though he looked and sounded awful."

"He coughed all night, though," Annie added. "I suggested he should stay another day with us, but he insisted on leaving bright and early, saying something about how the mail had to be delivered on time."

There was a long, worried pause. Then Mr. Andrews looked up into the evening sky. The sun was already setting.

"Ay," he finally said, "there's nothing to be done for it now. It's much too late to attempt the journey tonight, and you wouldn't be able to see anything along the way anyway. Come in for a bite to eat, and you can set off again tomorrow morning. Maybe Hamilton decided to take Annie's advice and rest up at the New River house." Even Mr. Andrews, however, didn't sound like he believed what he was saying.

After half a day walking in the hot sun, it was nice to walk into the cool, dark, and familiar interior of the house. The main floor was dominated by four big rooms, including a kitchen, living room, dining room, and bedroom. Upstairs, there was a dormitory for sailors and visitors. I could see the kitchen through the open door and saw that Mrs. Andrews—Annie, I corrected myself—had stoked a fire in the big iron stove and had full pots cooking on top.

While we ate, Mr. Andrews and Annie did their best to reassure us there was probably nothing to worry about, that Hamilton was most likely fine and probably had stopped to rest up. But I could tell they were worried too.

After dinner, I think hoping to take our minds off it, Mr. Andrews offered to show us some of his most recent finds. In addition to keeping the House of Refuge, one of his hobbies was collecting sea animals for the Smithsonian. Lillie perked up when we followed him into one of the empty bedrooms and saw the walls covered with all manner of strange and fantastic things. There were swords three feet long from swordfish as big as me and turtle shells with the dried barnacles still stuck on them, big enough for a full-grown man to use as a bathtub. On one wall, Mr. Andrews had hung six jagged sails from sailfish he had caught, and a jar on a shelf was full of glittering silvery discs that came from tarpon fish the size of donkeys.

"But this is really the pride of my collection right now," he said.

He crossed to a low table and picked up a white jawbone from a shark that was big enough to put my head through it, with razor-sharp teeth that sent my imagination spinning.

"What kind of shark is it?" I asked. "Did you catch it yourself?"

"Well, funny story that," Mr. Andrews said. "I didn't catch it, actually, but it was the most incredible thing. I'm afraid no one will believe me, but it was killed by a pod of dolphins just offshore. I watched from the beach. The shark was chasing the youngest dolphin, and then a whole pod of adult dolphins materialized and attacked all at once. The whole thing was over in seconds, and the shark washed up on shore not long after. Twelve foot long, it was. A bull shark."

"Dolphins!" Lillie said excitedly. "I wish I'd seen that!"

"It was truly amazing, Ms. Lillie," Mr. Andrews said. "And it makes me glad I live on the land, if you catch my meaning. Between the sharks, rays, and all sort of poisonous urchins, the sea looks plenty too dangerous for my taste."

He had meant it as a joke, but I could tell from Lillie's face that she was thinking the same thing as me: The land was plenty dangerous too.

I was already looking forward to getting an early start the next morning and hoping that we'd find Hamilton just like Mr. Andrews said—resting in the New River House of Refuge, the mail pouch sitting safely by his feet.

Chapter Seven

Nagging Doubt

We were up early the next day and ate a quick breakfast of Annie's pancakes and honey. After breakfast, we said our good-byes and were getting ready to go when Mr. Andrews said, "Hold on there for a moment, if you would."

Lillie and I looked at each other and shrugged.

Mr. Andrews disappeared into the room full of marine animals and emerged with a short brass tube. I recognized it at once, even as he snapped his wrist and expanded it into a short spyglass. He extended it toward me.

"For me?" I said. "What's this for?"

"I thought it might come in handy, you know, to help you see more of the landscape," he said. "I know you'll be careful with it. It's not a toy."

I took the heavy instrument carefully and

slid it shut. It had been oiled and smelled faintly of brass. I opened it back up and looked through the front door, down the beach. Trees and shrubs hundreds of yards away snapped into focus, seemingly so close that I felt if I reached out, I could actually touch their leaves.

"Can I see?" Lillie said.

I handed it over to her, and she held it up to her eye. "Wow!" she exclaimed, sweeping her view up the beach and adjusting the focus. "It looks like it's just a few inches away!"

"Thank you," I said to Mr. Andrews. "Are you sure?"

Mr. Andrews nodded. "Indeed, I am. Good luck, Charlie and Lillie. Go find Mr. Hamilton and make sure he's safe."

"Yes, sir," I said, and once again, I had a moment of confusion and conflicted feelings. I pushed the unpleasant thoughts away. "Thank you, we'll take good care of it."

"See that you do," he said. "Off with you now. It's fourteen miles to the inlet. You'll need to make good time. Keep your eyes open."

"Okay," I said as Lillie and I headed out. Bandit materialized by her side as we climbed down the steps. His whiskers were wet and sandy, and I suspected he had been digging for crabs along the beach.

It was very early and the sun was still rising over the Atlantic. Just like yesterday, the sea was calm and glowed golden green in the dawn light. Far offshore, enormous clouds shined orange and pink as the sun warmed their flanks. As we walked along, we saw big silver fish streaking through the foam, running close to the shallows and chasing minnows almost onto dry land.

We walked the first half hour in silence, lost in our thoughts. Every so often, Lillie lifted the spyglass to her eye and swept from horizon to horizon, scanning the thick sea grapes on the dune for any sign of Hamilton.

"Lillie?" I asked. "Can I ask you something, and you swear you won't get angry?"

She lowered the spyglass and gave me a sidelong look.

"Well," I started when she didn't answer, but then I stopped. I didn't even know how to put my suspicions into words. "Truth is, I feel like this is something I shouldn't even be thinking, much less saying, because Hamilton is a good friend of ours. He's helped us plenty of times before, and sure, he's new down here and all, but everybody's always liked him."

Lillie frowned but held her silence.

I went on, "So…well, I didn't even want to think this—"

"Stop right now," Lillie said crossly. "If you're

about to say you think Hamilton is already… dead and that we're wasting our time, I don't want to hear it. Not one bit, Charlie."

I shook my head. "That's not what I was about to say."

Lillie looked confused. "Then what were you going to say?"

"You know those plans he's carrying would be worth a lot of money to Mr. Gleason, and…well, you heard it yourself. He's new here, and Papa said his farm isn't making any money. Hamilton himself said he needed the money. So all of a sudden, here he is, finding himself in possession of the one thing Mr. Gleason needs to make himself very rich. You heard what Papa said, if a man was to find out where Mr. Flagler's railroad was supposed to go, and let's say that man had—"

"You stop that!" Lillie exclaimed, and I cut myself short, surprised.

"All I'm saying is that—"

"I mean it!" Lillie said, louder and angrier. Down near the water, Bandit lifted his head up and gave her a look. "If you're about to say you think Hamilton stole the mail and sold those plans to Mr. Gleason, then I don't want to hear one more word. Not one! We came all this way to find him and rescue him, not to accuse him of something as terrible as that."

A hundred things to say hopped into my head—including the fact that Lillie sounded exactly like Mama, and that I thought at least part of why Lillie was so mad had to do with her crush on Hamilton—but I kept my mouth shut. Because part of me knew she was right: I was being the worst sort of friend, and I cringed to think how I would feel if any of my own friends had harbored these kinds of suspicions about me. Yet still, I couldn't help the kernel of doubt.

Lillie gave me an angry look. "I can't believe you, Charlie," she said when I stayed quiet. "I really can't. I don't think I want to walk with you just now."

With that, she jogged ahead twenty yards and headed toward the beach dune, the spyglass raised to her eye as she scanned for any sign of our missing friend.

Chapter Eight

The Ominous Inlet

The rest of the morning was quiet. Neither of us mentioned the argument the rest of the long walk south. I wasn't sure if I was feeling guilty for accusing Hamilton of stealing the plans or annoyed with Lillie for defending Hamilton without really listening to me. Sometimes I felt both things at once. And all the time, I was worried about him.

We ended up making good time down the beach, hardly stopping for a tense lunch of hard biscuits. As the afternoon wore on, I found myself more and more wanting to make peace with Lillie, but she made herself almost impossible to talk to. Every time I started to speak, she'd cut me off with something like, "I don't want to talk about this anymore," or she'd find an excuse to dart up the dune or down toward the water.

Finally, after hours of walking in grumpy silence, we spotted the graceful coconut palms that marked the Hillsboro Inlet. We quickened our pace.

As we got nearer, I got a good look at the inlet. The Hillsboro Inlet was a hook-shaped cut in the beach that allowed the Hillsboro River and all of its little creeks to flow out into the Atlantic. It was a broad inlet but not a deep one. When the tide was low, a sandbar at the mouth of the inlet made it impossible to get upstream in anything except a canoe. You could walk most of the way across the inlet in knee-deep water—not that you'd want to. Even during low tide, there was a deep channel in the middle where the current could be strong.

Even with the sandbar, sailors liked the inlet because it was the best place to take cover from the weather for miles in either direction. If the tide was up, you could sail a decent-sized craft around the point and up the winding river channel. You'd quickly find yourself in a narrow, protected waterway clogged with mangrove and tree roots. If you managed to get far enough upstream, you'd find a little brackish lake where I'd sometimes fished for snook during the spring months.

I don't know what I was hoping to see as we got closer—maybe Hamilton sitting with his back to a coconut tree and his feet sticking out in front of him—but my heart sunk. I snuck a glance at Lillie. She looked upset.

The inlet was running as high as I'd ever seen it, with churning brown water rushing and hissing over the sand. The heavy summer rains over Pa-Hay-Okee must have flooded the swamp and sent sheets of water spreading across the land and toward the sea. When that happened, it was like opening up a dam, swelling every creek and river with rainwater and turning even little steams into fast-flowing rivers.

"I don't see the boat," Lillie said. "If he came back up this way, shouldn't the boat be on the north shore?"

"Yes, I guess it should," I said.

This was even worse news. Under normal circumstances, there should have been a boat waiting for us on the north shore. This boat was owned by the U.S. Postal Service, and it was supposed to be left there so the mailmen could get across the inlet. If Hamilton had followed his normal path, he would have used the boat to cross the inlet, left it on the south bank, and then used it to cross the inlet again as he headed back north on the return trip.

But it took only a glance through the spyglass across the inlet to see the boat on the south shore. This could only mean one thing: Hamilton had made it south but never come back north. Maybe he was holed up at the New River House of Refuge after all.

Lillie looked at me worriedly. "What should we do, Charlie? No way we can swim the inlet like this."

She was right. Not only was the inlet

running fast and high, I also recognized the dark outlines lying on the opposite shore farther upstream: alligators. As I watched, a ten-footer slid into the water and disappeared beneath the surface.

"Gators," I said. "The rain must have washed them down the river from Pa-Hay-Okee."

Lillie groaned. "What are we going to do?" she asked again. "We can't just turn around and go home."

Before I could answer, I heard a noise behind me and turned around. Bandit was in the coconut grove, standing on his hind legs and clawing at a trunk, stopping only to sniff at the wood. He stared up into the branches, but I didn't see anything up there. I was wondering what the little varmint was up to when an idea hit me, almost like Bandit had been trying to tell me something.

"Look," I said. "The ground is littered with branches back there. We could make a raft. If we were far enough upstream and away from the inlet, we could get across before the current washed us out into the ocean."

Lillie was looking at me like I'd lost my mind or started speaking French. "Are you serious?"

"Well," I said, "like you said, it's either that or turn around and go home."

She chewed on her lip and glanced at the

water, then back at the coconut grove. She nodded. "Okay," she said. "We better get started then."

We had no trouble finding all manner of downed branches and logs on the edge of the forest. We picked only the straightest and strongest of branches, dragging them into a big pile. Once we had enough, we lined them up on the sand, then went back into the jungle looking for something to use as rope. We'd hardly walked fifty feet when we came across a huge banyan tree with its roots hanging almost all the way to the ground. Lillie stuck my knife in her belt and scampered up the big tree to slice away long braids of thick root. Next, we knitted the braids together into long pieces of "rope" and wove the logs and branches together as best we could, going up and over and up and over until the collection of loose logs and branches looked like a raft.

"That's not too bad," I said, standing back to admire our work. "If we put a sail on this, we'd have a proper craft."

Lillie grinned at me, and I was happy to see her looking cheerful again.

"But seeing as how we don't have a sail," I said, smiling back at her, "we'll need a good long pole. I'm thinking we can drag the SS *Pierce* into the water, push upstream and pole our way across."

"The SS *Pierce*," she said. "That's funny, Charlie."

We soon found a straight ironwood branch and pulled the heavy raft toward the water. The current looked stronger up close, and the water was a worrisome brown where it had churned up the bottom. I tried to push away thoughts of what might be lurking below the surface as Lillie helped me shove our raft into the water.

"It floats!" she said happily as the raft bobbed in the current.

"Climb on," I said, more nervous than I wanted to let on. It had seemed like a good idea at first, but now that the raft was in the water, it looked like a small and flimsy contraption. And the water looked like it was moving even faster than I remembered. If we flipped over in the middle of the river, we'd end up washed out the inlet into the open ocean. And that was if things went well. If things went bad…I eyed the alligators lying in the sun upstream and tried to not think about that.

Bandit was the last to hop on the raft as I stuck the pole in the sandy shore and pushed us off. The first few feet were easy enough, and I was just starting to hope that we'd make an easy crossing when the current grabbed the little raft, and we started to spin like a leaf caught in a whirlpool. Lillie shouted as I dug the pole into the bottom to stop the spinning and tried to force us across the swollen river.

But it didn't seem like a winning battle. For every foot we went across the river, it seemed like we were swept ten feet downstream toward the mouth of the inlet. I was so distracted, I hardly noticed when one of the big alligators upstream slid from the bank into the water and disappeared.

"Charlie!" Lillie yelled. "We've got to go faster!"

She grabbed the pole with me, and together we pushed so hard that the branch bent and creaked. I was afraid it would break, but instead it sprang back, and we gained another few precious feet across the river. By now, we were almost in the middle, and the water was splashing up through the logs around our feet. The lashings had come undone in a few places.

The next time I stuck the pole in the water, I almost toppled over. It was too deep to reach the bottom. We were shooting down the middle of the river and starting to spin again. The far bank seemed a hundred miles away.

"Paddle!" I yelled at Lillie.

She was already ahead of me and had dropped to her knees on the edge of the raft and was paddling at the water with both hands. Bandit was chattering anxiously and darting from edge to edge. I fell to my knees and plunged my hands into the water to paddle furiously.

It didn't take long to realize we weren't going to make it. Another minute and I reckoned we'd be in the main mouth of the inlet, getting

pushed out to sea. I knew from experience that the current from an outgoing river like this could be very strong. We might be pushed a half mile offshore before it let us go, meaning we'd have to jump off and swim for it. But that didn't sound too great either; getting caught in an ocean current could be deadly.

I knew what I had to do. I glanced at Lillie, who was still paddling, and then I looked up at the alligators sunning themselves on the shore. A few more had disappeared into the water. My heart started to pound, but I didn't let myself dwell on it. I wrapped a loose strand of our homemade rope around my wrist and slipped into the warm water. The current grabbed my body and tried to pull me away from our little raft, but I clung to the rope.

"Charlie!" Lillie yelled. "What are you doing?"

I started to kick for everything I was worth. I couldn't be sure I was making progress, and every second lasted forever as I imagined the gators coming up from beneath me in the brown water. My lungs felt like they would burst and my legs ached, but I kept kicking and kicking.

And then all of a sudden, the pull of the current slacked off. We had cleared the channel in the middle of the river! With a few more kicks, I felt for the bottom and was flooded with relief when my foot dug into soft sand. A minute later, Lillie and I dragged ourselves onto the sandy beach on the south shore, breathing hard. We let the raft go, and it bobbed down the shoreline, heading for the open sea.

"Whew," Lillie said, almost laughing with relief. "I wouldn't want to do that again."

I shook my head as my breathing calmed. "No way. Not sure I *could* do that again."

We sat panting for a minute as the sun dried my skin. When my heart finally had slowed down, I sat up and looked at my sister. She was already on her feet and had the spyglass out, scanning the beach and the south shore of the river. "Good thing those gators weren't hungry," she said lightly.

"Don't remind me," I said. "So you ready? We've still got miles to cover to get to the next House of Refuge."

She snapped the spyglass closed. "Yep. C'mon, Bandit, let's go find our friend."

Chapter Nine

The New River House of Refuge

Maybe it was the excitement of the river crossing, or maybe it was the salty taste of the brackish water still in my mouth, but within an hour of crossing the inlet, I was seized with a powerful thirst. Unfortunately, we didn't have any water left—we had filled our canteens when we left the Orange Grove house—but it was already late afternoon, and we had walked miles and miles under the hot sun.

Things between Lillie and me had seemed okay right after the crossing, but it wasn't long before the subject of Hamilton came up again. I didn't want to fight with her, but neither did I want to take back what I had said. "You don't know for certain what happened," I reminded Lillie. "You might think you do, but you don't. You might know the woods and animals as well as anyone, but that don't mean you know people and what they're capable of when it comes to money."

"*Doesn't* mean," she said, correcting me with a triumphant look. "It *doesn't* mean I know people. And for your information, I think I know people a lot better than you do."

"What if you're wrong, Lillie?" I said, frustrated. "What if Hamilton and Gleason are just now sitting down at his house and plotting ways to make themselves rich through blackmail? What if that railroad doesn't come down here at all because of it? Or, what if it does come down here, but this time Gleason has enough money and power to really throw us off our land? I bet you would never admit you were wrong."

Lillie snorted. "Listen to yourself, Charlie. You're just about the most paranoid person I've ever heard. What if the moon fell from the sky tonight and squashed our island? What if a giant whale washed up on shore and gobbled us up? What if, what if, what if."

"Now you're just being stubborn," I said angrily.

"Same for you. I'd like to hear you say you're sorry when you're wrong." Her voice broke, and I realized she was near tears. "The worst part is… for all we know our friend is in real trouble, and all you can think about is the most underhanded, terrible thing you can think."

"You know what I don't understand? How you can be so sure of the character of a person who's only been down here for eighteen months. I think I know why, and it's got nothing to do with whether he's a good person or not. It's because you're just sweet on him."

"Charlie!" Lillie said in a pained voice. "You're being awful."

I fell into a moody silence and tried to pretend that my insides weren't being gnawed on by guilt and doubt. But darn it, I told myself, I was right, and anyway, I wouldn't have said what I said if Lillie hadn't provoked me.

"Lillie!" I finally called out when my tongue felt like a fuzzy caterpillar in my mouth. "Hey, Lillie!"

She was walking ten yards or so ahead, still scanning the horizon every few minutes with the spyglass. She turned her head over her shoulder. "What?" she said.

"Remember that thing you showed Hamilton? With the coconuts?"

"Yeah, I remember."

"You think you could show me? I feel like I might fall over from thirst any second."

"Why shouldn't I just let you?"

"Because then you wouldn't have a brother anymore."

She rolled her eyes. "Oh fine," she said. "Come on."

She took me up the beach to the dune, where the occasional coconut tree leaned forward over the sand. These were tall coconuts, with a spray of fronds way up high and trunks that grew almost parallel to the ground before turning up and shooting skyward. Lillie walked along, her head turned up to inspect the trees.

"Okay," she said, standing at the base of a healthy looking coconut tree. "Watch."

She took my knife and slid it into her waistband, then removed a short length of braided banyan root from her pocket. She looped one end around her wrist, then jumped up lightly onto a coconut palm. She walked along the trunk like a tightrope walker until she got to the bend.

"Here's what you do," she said, looping the braid around the trunk and grabbing it with her other hand. "You lean back against the rope, see? And jump up a few feet, then grab the trunk with the insides of both feet. It's best if your feet are bare. It takes a little bit to get the feel for it, but once you do, you just keep moving the rope up the trunk and leaning back, then jumping with both feet."

"You mean sort of like a monkey?" I said, smiling.

"Very funny," she said. "Do you want a drink or not?"

"No, go ahead."

She did just as she said, jumping up a few feet and leaning back against the braided length of banyan rope. Then, so quick I could scarcely believe it, she scampered up the straight, smooth trunk. I craned my neck, following her progress far out over the sand and high up into the tree. When she reached a cluster of nuts, I was surprised to see how big they were next to her head: Each coconut was bigger than a cannonball. She gripped the trunk with her legs, reached back to get the knife, and cut a few loose. They came thudding down to the ground, sloshing coconut milk inside them. My mouth started watering even before Lillie slid back down to the ground.

"See?" she said. "Even you could do that if you needed to."

I let that one go as she used the knife to bore two holes into the thick green rind of the first nut and handed it to me. I greedily let the sweet, clear liquid pour into my mouth while she prepared the second coconut and took a drink herself.

"Thanks," I said.

She shrugged. "Next time you can get your own."

I almost had a retort but decided we'd fought enough for one day. "C'mon," I said. "We're almost there."

***

We made the New River House of Refuge just as dark settled over the land. The bats were out, swooping through the warm night air and gorging themselves on mosquitoes. The wind had picked up, so I could hear the surf hissing on the shore, but there still wasn't enough breeze to blow the pesky mosquitoes away.

We were nearly asleep on our feet by the time we were greeted by the New River keeper, Jolly Jack Peacock, and his wife. Jolly Jack was a huge man who reminded me of every pirate drawing I'd ever seen, minus the eye patch. He had a big voice and big smile to match and boomed his hello like we were long-lost relatives. I was more than happy to return the greeting. In all, we had walked about twenty miles since dawn, and my legs felt every step of it. Of course, we asked right away about Hamilton.

"I'm sorry," Jolly Jack said, his face falling. "But he hasn't been here at all. We've been more than a bit worried. Not like a mail carrier to skip the New River."

"But the boat was on the south shore," Lillie protested. "He must have come by here."

Jolly Jack just shook his head. "No, he never came."

I lay in bed later that night, listening to the drone of waves and thinking. It's true we'd been distracted after the crossing, but not so

much that we would have missed Hamilton along the beach. And it didn't make sense that he would have crossed the dune to go into the woods. The stretch of land between the Hillsboro Inlet and the New River House of Refuge was particularly marshy. Nobody in their right mind would wade into that swamp without a good reason.

I remembered the alligators along the shore, and a shiver ran through me. But then I reminded myself the boat was on the south shore. No, he must have crossed the river and headed south, bypassing the New River House of Refuge for some reason known only to himself.

When I finally fell asleep, I felt like I was plunging into a mystery that kept growing deeper with every step.

Chapter Ten

Our First Fizzies

We got an early start the next morning—it promised to be another long day walking along the beach. We'd get to the New River before lunch. I wondered what we'd find when we got there.

I found out an hour or so later when the river came into view: the U.S. Postal boat was sitting on the north shore, just where it was supposed to be. Lillie and I glanced at each other and scanned the beach and dune.

"You think we missed him?" she said. "Maybe?"

"I don't know how we could have."

"But if this boat is on the north shore and the other boat is on the south shore—"

"I know. He either didn't make it this far south or someone came back north and used it. Might not even have been him."

"That doesn't help."

"No, it doesn't," I agreed.

"So what do you reckon we do?" she asked. "Turn around? Keep going south?"

I sighed and thought, standing on the riverbank and looking around. The New River was broader than the Hillsboro Inlet and running fast and high, its banks clogged with mangrove trees and thick jungle. Royal palm trees towered over the landscape. My friend Tiger Bowlegs said they called it the New River because according to the Seminole legend, one day the ground shook and a terrible wind blew, and the next day a river appeared where there had been no river before.

I wasn't sure if I believed the Seminole story, but I was thankful we had the boat—trying to cross this fast river on a homemade raft would have been impossible.

"Well," I finally said, "I guess we keep going south. See if he ever showed up at the Brickell place or Biscayne House of Refuge, then come back north. If we turn back now, we'd be turning around with no more answers than we had sitting at home."

Lillie nodded in agreement.

We made the crossing with no problem and were soon heading south again. The land grew wilder and the jungle thicker the farther south we headed. Little rivers and streams cut the dune more frequently, trickling across the beach and staining the Atlantic where the brown river water mixed with the pure ocean green. The dune ridge was high here, but I knew what the land was like on the other side: laced with streams too numerous to name that shifted course depending on the rain and wind, and a seemingly endless network of bogs and swamps dotted with higher pineland and soggy jungle hammocks, everything infested with all manner of reptiles and biting insects. It would have been impossible to navigate this treacherous terrain on foot.

Every so often, we'd pass signs of the people who once had lived here: a random post dug into the sand for a marker, some soot-stained rocks stacked into fire rings or broken chimneys.

Papa had told me about these settlers—they'd lived here forty years or more earlier, but everybody had fled after the Seminole War. Major William Lauderdale had built a fort here, but that was deserted too. Now there was no one left in this dense and steaming forest except for the birds and animals.

We saw no sign of Hamilton as the miles spooled away beneath our feet and we talked about all manner of things. We stopped for a lunch of hard biscuits and water, then hurried on our way. I think we had silently agreed not to fight anymore, and I was grateful for that.

Instead of following the normal route, we made a quick decision after lunch to pass Baker's Haulover at the head of Biscayne Bay, where another boot usually waited to sail the mailman down the bay to the Brickell place, and instead head for the Biscayne Bay House of Refuge. The mail carriers didn't normally go this way, but we hoped there was a chance Hamilton was there. It was a long shot, we agreed, but worth a try. Moreover, we were afraid of using a U.S. Postal Service boat to sail Biscayne Bay. Crossing the New River was one thing, but taking a boat all the way down the bay felt too close to stealing.

The Biscayne Bay House of Refuge was located on the east shore of Biscayne Bay on a spit of land between the bay and ocean. I hardly was surprised to learn from the keeper, Mr. William Fulford, that Hamilton hadn't been seen here either. He suggested we borrow one of his boats and press on down the bay to the Brickell place, to see if they had any more information.

We soon shoved away from the beach on the little sailboat Mr. Fulford had loaned us. He kept two of these little boats always on the bayside so people could easily make the trip from his House of Refuge down the bay. After walking for two days, neither Lillie nor I was sorry to be on a boat.

It was an uneventful trip down to the Brickell trading post, where it squatted on a point of land at the place where the Miami River spilled into Biscayne Bay. The Miami River was also swollen and running fast, washing brown silt and weeds into the bay. As we approached the Brickell place, I glanced at

Lillie. She was studying the big white building, her eyebrows creased. Since last time we'd come, they'd built a big Seminole chickee hut near to the point, and a smaller building peeked through the trees farther inland.

"Look," she said. "I wonder who that is?"

She was staring at a small one-masted boat tied up along the big dock.

I shrugged. The Brickell place was the main trading post in Miami. It was a popular spot to get supplies for anyone sailing down to the Keys or up north along the coast—pretty much anyone traveling through these parts would stop here at one time or another. It wouldn't be unusual to find several boats here at any given time.

"I guess we'll find out soon enough," I said, waving as Mary Brickell came out of the trading post, hailing us and preparing to take our ropes. It had been a while since I'd seen Mrs. Brickell, and I was once again struck by her appearance. She was of medium height, with short hair that she had parted straight down the middle of her head. She had a broad face with large eyes that glittered with a fierce intelligence as she waited for Lillie and me to climb out of the boat.

"Well, hello there," she said, smiling. "I'm guessing it's been six months since we last saw you down this way? You're both growing so quickly. And how are your parents? I heard your Pa was bitten by a snake?"

"Yes, ma'am," I said, marveling at how fast

news traveled, even down to here. "He's better now, though. He's getting around just fine."

"Good to hear," she said, coming forward to shake our hands. She gripped my hand with a strong handshake—it reminded me of Papa's saying that he could always tell the measure of a man by his handshake, except that Mrs. Brickell wasn't a man at all. "So what can we do for you? You kids headed down farther south?"

 "No, actually we came here looking for the new mail carrier, Mr. Hamilton," I said. "He should have been here a week ago and left already."

Her eyes narrowed a little bit, and she glanced over my shoulder. "Why no," she finally said.

"We haven't seen him at all, and likewise, haven't received any mail. Seems that half of South Florida is on the lookout for him, though."

Before I could ask what she meant by that, she smiled and turned. "Now come on inside," she said. "We just got a brand-new soda fountain, and I've been waiting for just the right customers to help me break it in."

We followed her inside the big two-story building. The first floor of the Brickell trading post was stocked with every kind of implement and material you'd need to live in these parts. There were sacks of flour and rice stacked up along the wall, a display case with knives and guns, cases of dynamite marked CAUTION, and bins full of rope, fishing gear, blankets, and sail cloth. A staircase in the back ran up to the rooms above, and I knew you could rent a room for a night or two if you needed a place to stay and didn't have a boat to sleep on. They also had a few tables and a big open counter.

Mostly, my eyes were instantly drawn to the soda fountain behind the counter. I'd never seen anything quite like it. The machine had an arrangement of tubes and cylinders with bottles of brightly colored syrup lined up along the wall next to it. There was a spout too with a big handle sticking up.

Next to me, Lillie looked just as curious about the contraption neither of us had ever seen before but only read about in Mama's magazines.

Still, I didn't want to forget why we were there.

"So you're saying he never came here in the past two weeks?" I said as Mrs. Brickell went behind the counter and pulled down two glasses.

"No," she said. "We thought about sending word up north to see if he'd been waylaid, but there's been a pretty steady stream of people through here asking about him, not least of all your Uncle Will, who was here just a few days ago. He was the one who told us about your Papa's snake bite and that sugarcane. Sounds like you're getting ready to harvest?"

"Yes, ma'am," I said.

She set the glasses on the counter. "Well, good luck to you all, and good luck to anyone looking for Hamilton. It's serious business when a man goes missing down here, especially if he's the man with the mail."

"Yes, ma'am."

"Now," she said, "what flavor you want? This here is a real carbonic soda machine. For flavor, we've got strawberry, cream soda, and root beer."

"Root beer," Lillie said immediately, and I picked strawberry. We watched with fascination as she pulled the handle and poured a stream of syrup into the gushing, fizzy liquid that rushed out. It was cold, and when I put it up to my face to drink, I almost sneezed from the bubbles hopping off the surface of the drink. Still, that first sip was a revelation. It was fizzy all right, like a ball of strawberry-flavored static electricity that lit up my mouth and nose and tingled all the way down my throat. Lillie looked every bit as impressed as I was, and it seemed like only a minute had passed before we both drained our glasses. Mrs. Brickell smiled broadly as we set our empty glasses back on the counter.

"So," she said, "you came all this way to find Hamilton? When was the last time anyone heard from him?"

I was just starting to tell her the whole story

when shadows fell across the shop as three men entered the trading post. She looked up and frowned. I looked back to see Mr. Brickell coming in through the door, followed by two men I'd never seen before. He glanced at his wife, and a strange look passed between them.

I wondered why they looked so worried.

Chapter Eleven

Trouble Shows Up

The men walking in behind Mr. Brickell looked like the rough sort. They were wearing leather vests and had a week's worth of stubble on their cheeks. They wore dirty old hats with broken rims, and unlike any of the men I knew around South Florida, both of them were wearing holsters around their waists. The taller of the two had a pistol in his, but the shorter man's holster was empty. The taller of the two mopped his face with a bandanna. "I don't know how you tolerate this heat," he said. "Feels like it could melt a volcano out there."

"You get used to it," Mr. Brickell said mildly. Then he noticed us. "Why, if it isn't Charlie and Lillie Pierce! Nice to see you. Looks like you're getting acquainted with our new soda machine. What'd you think?"

"It's great," I said. "I've never had anything like it before."

"We're just down here looking—" Lillie started.

But Mrs. Brickell cut her off. "So you two boys are taken care of then? I'm guessing you'll be spending the night on your boat before heading back up north?"

"Unless you want to give us proper beds in one of them upstairs rooms," the sweaty tall man said.

"No, I'm sorry," she said firmly. "We aren't a hotel. That's private living quarters up there."

"Shame," he said. He looked at his partner. "Looks like the whole trip's been wasted. Thanks for showing us around, though. This is an impressive spread you've got here, considering you live on the edge of this godforsaken swamp."

Neither of the Brickells answered that, and an uncomfortable silence drew out.

"Alright then," the tall man said. "I guess we'll be heading out to the boat then. Shove off tomorrow morning. We'll need a few things before then, but I suppose we can handle that later."

"That sounds fine," Mrs. Brickell said in a cold voice, and the two men turned around and headed back outside, leaving us with the two Brickells in their shop.

"Who were they?" I asked. "I never seen them around here before."

"They're down from Georgia," Mr. Brickell

answered. "And the sooner they head back up that way, the better."

Speaking to her husband, Mrs. Brickell nodded at us. "The Pierce children came down looking for Hamilton. Said he left their place up in Hypoluxo nearly two weeks ago, and no one has seen him since."

Mr. Brickell's mouth tightened. "Is that so?"

"Yes, sir. We were hoping to get some news of him down here, but…I guess not," Charlie said.

"No, Charlie, I'm sorry we can't help you." He paused. "I wish we could, though. I guess you'll be staying here the night?"

"Yes, sir. Don't worry. We plan on sleeping on the boat. We borrowed it from Mr. Fulford up at the House of Refuge, and I don't want to leave it unattended during the night."

"You sure are good kids," he said. "And so you know, we'll be right in here if you need us. Just give a shout."

"Sure, thanks."

Lillie and I spent the rest of the afternoon hanging around in the trading post, heading outside every so often to fish off the dock. Mr. Brickell said there were big tarpon living under his dock, but we never managed to entice anything out except for a few crabs and sheepshead. The two rough-looking men stayed on their boat all afternoon, sitting on the deck with their feet up and their hats pulled low over their eyes. One of them had a fishing pole with a chunk of pork fat dangling in the water. I had no idea what he was trying to catch with pork fat, but he looked more interested in the brown bottle that he and his partner passed back and forth all afternoon.

As the sun went down, we ate inside with the Brickells and told them all about the sugarcane mill and Papa's plan to start making lots of sugar. Mrs. Brickell promised us she'd be first in line once we had enough sugar to sell. Finally, with the darkness coming up, Lillie and I bid our hosts a good-night and went outside to the boat.

The two men were nowhere to be seen.

"Charlie," Lillie said, "you're not worried about those two tonight, are you?"

"Why would I be worried?" I asked. "We got the Brickells right here. And we'll be on our boat. Nobody would bother two kids on a boat."

"I know. It's just…they're carrying pistols. You think they're deputies maybe?"

This was a new thought to me, and my suspicion of Hamilton flashed back through my head. What if they were down here trying to apprehend Hamilton for stealing the mail. But then…

"I don't think so," I said. "They had no badges. And every deputy I've ever seen was clean-shaven and respectable looking. Those two were anything but."

Lillie nodded. "I know what you mean."

Because it was so hot, we planned to sleep on the deck and set up the mosquito netting and bed rolls. We were lying on the deck and Lillie was pointing out stars and constellations a short while later when I heard voices and sat up. I saw a light flare to life down the shore a ways, toward the point. It was the two men from earlier. They weren't on their boat after all but sitting crowded around a small, smoky fire of green wood near the shore.

I was just wondering if we should explore—I had a strange feeling about those two men, even if I couldn't explain exactly why—when Lillie said, "We should go see what they're talking about."

"You took the words out of my mouth," I said. "You got a feeling about them too?"

"Yeah," she said. "And there's no law that we can't take a walk at night."

"S'long as we stay hidden," I said.

A minute later, we were creeping down the dock toward the point. We stayed in the shadows, but it wouldn't have mattered anyway. They were a ways away from the end of the dock, facing the water with their backs to us. I saw the brown flash of a bottle passing between them, and they weren't making any effort to lower their voices. We stopped by a big piling near the end of the dock and stood still like statues to catch their voices. It wasn't hard, as their voices carried easily over the water.

"So now what?" the shorter man said to his partner. "Like I been saying, we better not go back empty-handed."

"I'm thinking."

"I still don't know how he managed to get away like that. You'd think a man wouldn't be able to up and vanish with the two of us after him like that."

The taller man took a drink from the bottle. "Maybe it's something new they're teaching in mailman school."

Lillie took a sharp breath next to me, and I went slightly numb. Mailman school?

"You know what really worries me?" the tall man said, passing the bottle back.

"What'll happen to us when we get back without them plans?" the other said.

"Nah," the tall man said. "I ain't worried about Gleason. He's a politician like the rest of 'em. No, it's the law what worries me the most."

"The law? Why would we have anything to fear from the law?"

"What'll happen when that mailman shows back up from wherever he is? He got a good look at us. And it didn't help none that you left your pistol back at the inlet somewhere. How you think it's gonna look when he shows up with your pistol and that story?" When his partner didn't answer, he continued, "I'll tell you how it'll look. None too good. We'll have to head back up to Georgia if it comes to that, Gleason or no Gleason."

The other man grunted. I was so distracted, my mind spinning so fast, that I almost didn't feel the slight tug on my sleeve. It was Lillie. Her face was white as a ghost, and she was pulling me back along the dock.

We crept back onto our boat.

"Did you hear that, Charlie?" she whispered urgently.

"Of course I did," I answered more sharply than I meant. Along with everything else, I was feeling guilty: I had been very wrong about Hamilton, and the truth was even worse than anything Lillie had imagined. Gleason had hired men to rob his own mail carrier!

"What are we gonna do, Charlie?" she asked. "I don't want to stay on the boat tonight."

"We're just a couple of kids," I said. "They won't bother with us. But…I'll tell you one thing. We're on our way at first light. You heard what he said about the inlet. Something happened there. We need to get back up there and figure out what it was."

Chapter Twelve

An Apology

We were awake with the gray dawn the next day. It was still and cool compared to the white-hot heat that was sure to follow. The surface of the bay was calm too, only rippling and surging where the big fish were hunting mullet and baitfish.

We didn't want to wake Mr. and Mrs. Brickell, so we prepared to shove off as silently as possible. I untied the boat and pushed us off from the dock with hardly a whisper. The other boat was still firmly tied up to the dock, and we had to pass within fifteen feet of it as we sailed away from the point. Lillie and I held our breath as we sliced through the clear water, the foam hissing away from our bow. Even Bandit seemed to be holding his breath and sat on his hind legs on the deck, watching. The two men were sleeping on the deck, their hats over the faces and their boots still on. My heart jumped into my throat when the tall man stirred as we went by, but then he settled down again.

As soon as we made the open water of the bay, we turned north toward the top of Biscayne Bay and fought for every breath of wind we could scavenge on the still morning. I tacked back and forth every few minutes, swinging the sail back and forth to keep it from going slack. I felt strongly we had to beat those men up to the inlet.

Lillie and I hardly said a word to each other as we sailed, but my mind was a welter of emotions and thoughts. Not only had I been wrong about Hamilton, but we also had information now that would have to get out. If Gleason was trying to steal those plans, it meant he knew all about the railroad and that he was willing to do anything to turn a profit from it, even hire gunmen.

"Lillie," I said quietly as the Biscayne Bay House of Refuge came into sight a while later.

"Yes, Charlie?"

I looked at her. "I owe you an apology. You said you didn't think I'd ever admit it if I was wrong, so here I am saying I was wrong."

She returned my look, and instead of the devilish grin I'd expected, she looked tired and frightened. "What do you think they did to him? Why would Gleason hire men like that?"

"I don't know," I said. "But here's what I'm thinking: If Gleason had to hire gunmen to steal the plans, it meant that Hamilton wouldn't part with them any other way. That says something about the kind of man he is and says how wrong I was."

"Now you sound just like Papa," she said.

I smiled.

"You think he's okay?" she asked. "What do you think we're looking for?"

"I don't know," I said honestly. "I just know that something happened at the inlet. Maybe if we can find that lost pistol ourselves, together with what we've heard here, we'd have enough to interest the law up in Tallahassee or Jacksonville."

She looked even more miserable and I wondered what I'd said wrong. "I don't care about interesting the law," she said. "I just want to find our friend. I hate the thought of him fighting those two off."

"Yeah, me too."

The wind picked up as the morning drew on, and we prepared to dock and drop the boat off. As we tied the lines up along Mr. Fulford's dock, I thought I saw a glint of a white sail back down the bay. For a moment, I worried that the two men had figured us out and were giving chase, but then the mirage disappeared, and I told myself I was seeing things.

The walk back up to the New River was the fastest march of our lives. We nearly ran up the beach, but it still felt like time was crawling and we couldn't get there fast enough. We ate lunch on our feet, passing our last hard biscuit back and forth and sipping water from a bottle Mrs. Brickell had given us. After ten miles on foot, we made the New River inlet in the mid-afternoon, when the sun stood straight overhead and the landscape seemed to broil under its merciless platinum light.

The boat was still on the south shore, half hidden in the thick jungle, so we rowed ourselves across the swollen river and pushed forward. We made another few miles before Lillie said, "We better stop for the night, Charlie. No sense in walking in the dark."

I agreed, and we used the last of the daylight to lash together a small campsite in the sea grapes that grew on the dune face. We made a quick roof of thatch and had a poor dinner of sea pickle, pigeon plum, and sea grapes. We huddled in our little shelter and looked out across the wide beach to the glittering ocean.

I slept poorly that night, waking over and over, thinking I heard footsteps on the beach or the jingle of a belt loaded with a pistol and ammunition. I lay with my head propped on my arm, watching the night birds and bats darting overhead and listening to the shush of water on the sand, thinking I was just being foolish and everything would look normal again in the daylight. But in the deepest part of the night, it was hard to shake the feeling that those two men were behind us somewhere, coming for us too.

Dawn did bring some relief, and even though I was tired, I was up with the first light and roused Lillie. Bandit was curled up next to her, and soon the three of us were heading up the beach again.

Chapter Thirteen

Bandit's Secret

We made the Hillsboro Inlet just after lunch, both of us with sweat streaming down our necks and tired. I figured it must have been the fastest walk north in the history of South Florida, but instead of calling for a rest, we hurried on when we saw the tall grove of coconut trees that marked the inlet.

Everything looked exactly as we left it, including the boat pulled up on the south shore.

"We should start on this shore," I said.

"Remember the boat was here when we got here. Maybe he got across…"

Lillie was a better tracker than me, so she headed up the inlet toward the thick jungle that choked its shores while I stuck to the bank and headed for the ocean. I didn't know what I was looking for exactly—a broken branch? footprints? the missing pistol?—but it didn't seem to matter anyway. The sand was washed clean from the summer rains, and if I wanted to find a broken branch, all I had to do was look a few feet in any direction. As for finding the pistol, the closest thing I found to any weapon at all was an old conch shell with a sharp point on it.

Frustrated, I headed back to the boat, only to find Lillie waiting for me. I could tell right away from the look on her face that she'd had no luck either.

"Nothing?" I asked.

"Nope, not even a print in the mud. Far as I can tell, no one has been up that way at all."

I sighed. "Okay, so let's cross and search the north shore. You heard what they said. *Something* happened here. Something."

"But what?" she asked.

"Beats me."

We climbed into the boat, and I shoved us off. Crossing the inlet this time was much easier, considering we just rowed our way across and soon bumped up against the sandy shore. Lillie hopped out and pulled the bow up enough that I could clamber out and pull the boat up onto the bank.

Because of the way the inlet was shaped, this side was much more open with a broad field on the hook-shaped piece of land. The east half of this field was dominated by the stand of mature coconut trees swaying gracefully in the breeze, while the west part of the little plain was overtaken with trees and thick plants that hid the river almost completely from sight.

"Should be a lot easier to find footprints here," Lillie said. "Why don't you go see if you can find the missing gun, and I'll look for prints."

I wandered off toward the rushing water's edge, my head down and every sense on high alert. Bandit raced ahead of me down to the water and then back past me toward the coconut grove. I ignored the pesky raccoon. A few minutes of searching didn't reveal anything, but I had this growing certainty that we were getting closer to finally finding a clue. We had walked all the way from Hypoluxo to Biscayne Bay and halfway back again without seeing any trace of Hamilton. A man couldn't simply disappear, no matter what the thugs at the Brickell place said.

There!

I froze in my tracks and stared hard at the ground by my feet. I was in a sandy area with old rotting palm fronds and branches covering the ground. I'd almost missed it, but one of the fronds was showing a strip of green where it had been bent recently. The sand beneath it was still clean and fresh.

I squatted and held my breath. Sure enough, there was no question this palm frond was bent. Of course, it could have been an animal, but then I looked up away from the river and saw an indentation in the sand that was too deep to be anything other than a human footprint.

Someone had been here!

And suddenly there it was as plain as day: a trail of old footprints on the cluttered ground. They were old, some filled in already with sand, and I couldn't tell if they were heading toward the water or away from the water. But it was something.

"Lillie!" I called out. "Lillie! Come here and look at this!"

My sister raced over and knelt beside me to inspect the ground, nodding and following the tracks.

"Look," she whispered. "Charlie! Look!"

At first I didn't see what was she pointing at in the shady coconut grove. There was nothing special there I could see, just Bandit—

Bandit!

The raccoon was up on his hind legs at the base of a tall coconut tree, scratching at the bark. All of a sudden, I had a memory of seeing Bandit doing exactly the same thing the first time we came this way. Back then, I had dismissed him, but now it occurred to me he had been trying to tell us something.

Lillie and I looked at each other and ran into the grove, careful not to disturb any footprints.

The trail disappeared once we got into the trees, but it felt like something was pulling us forward. Soon we stood at the base of the tree with Bandit, peering up into the huge fronds forty feet above the ground.

I still didn't see anything.

"Charlie," Lillie said slowly, "You don't think… you don't think he climbed up there, did he?"

"Why would he do that?" I asked. "When you showed him how to climb that morning, I never saw him make it more'n five feet up the trunk. This is a big tree."

"Let me see that spyglass," she said, holding out her hand.

I handed it to her, and she telescoped the lens and peered up into the branches. Then she caught her breath. "There's something up there! I can see it."

A minute later, Lillie had fashioned herself a short braid from palm fronds, taken off her shoes and was shimmying up the tree. I yelled at her to be careful as she made it first ten, then twenty, then thirty, and finally, all forty feet up into the crown of the tree. If she fell from that height, it could kill her.

"The pouch!" she called down, her face an excited oval above me. "It's the pouch!"

"Well, get it and bring it down!"

I held my breath while she gripped the trunk with her legs and reached up into the fronds. From below, the fronds looked small, but compared to Lillie, it was obvious how huge they really were. After a few nerve-racking seconds, she tugged hard and suddenly, almost magically, produced the familiar brown leather pouch with the words "U.S. MAIL" emblazoned on the side in white. She looped it around her neck and slid down the tree.

No sooner had she hit the ground than we crowded over the mail pouch while Bandit skittered excitedly around our feet.

I don't know what I expected to find, but it looked like the ordinary mail: letters, bundles of magazines, and a big white envelope tied with twine and the official state seal on it. I lifted it out. "These must be the plans," I said.

"But…it's just the mail," Lillie said in a frustrated voice. "Why on earth would he climb the tree to hide the mail like that? It doesn't make any sense."

I was about to answer when a chilling sound rang out from the nearby jungle—metal jangling.

We looked up and Bandit hissed, only to see the two thugs step out from behind a tree, both grinning.

"Well, well," the tall one said. "Lookee what we have here."

Chapter Fourteen

Lillie's Sprint

My heart leaped into my chest. I fought two impulses: the first to throw the mail pouch away from me as far as I could throw it and the second to grab Lillie and shove her behind me. Then I looked at Lillie and saw that stubborn look on her face. Uh-oh.

"Well, kiddies," the tall man said. "I guess you're going to want to hand over that pouch."

"What'd you do to our friend?" Lillie demanded.

The short man smiled in the same lazy sort of way I imagined a panther would smile before it jumped on a deer.

"The cub thinks she has teeth," he said.

"I mean it!" she said in a louder, angrier voice. "What did you do to him? You…you bad men!"

The taller one laughed and shook his head.

"Look, little girl, we didn't do nothing to him, okay? But we will do something to you if you don't hand over that pouch."

I stepped forward. "Now you wait," I said, my mind spinning. "What are you going to do? Hurt kids? Lots of people know we're here."

The tall man took a step closer to me, and I saw his eyes were red-rimmed, and he looked haggard under his stubble. It occurred to me they must have sailed all night to get here before us and lie in wait. I silently cursed our decision to stop for the night.

"I sincerely doubt anyone knows you're here," he said. "Anyway, it don't matter who knows what, because here at this moment on this piece of land, it's just you two and us."

"How'd you get here anyway?" I asked, stalling for time. "We left before you."

They glanced at each other. "Let's just say I had a feeling about you two, the way you hightailed it out of there first thing in the morning."

"You knew we had come looking for Hamilton?"

The tall man took a deep breath and sighed, then rubbed his stubbly chin. "Kid, I don't really want to stand around jawing all day with you. Just give over the pouch."

"Why?" Lillie said. "So you can give it to that snake Gleason?"

"Who?" the tall man said. "Never heard of him."

"You're lying," she said. "I can see it on your face. You're a liar. Did you hurt Hamilton?"

"Even if I told you, you just said I'm a liar. You wouldn't believe me none anyway. Now, this is the last time I'll ask nicely before I tell my partner here to come get it." The short man grinned, and I saw his teeth had mostly gone gray. "And trust me, his manners ain't nearly as good as mine."

"*Aren't* nearly," Lillie said. "They *aren't* nearly as good as yours."

The tall man's eyes narrowed as he worked this out, then his face twisted in a snarl when he realized she was insulting him. "C'mon, Carl," he growled. "Time for talking is done."

What happened next felt like slow motion. They both started forward, running in the strange sort of waddle of men who've spent most of their lives on horses. I grabbed for Lillie, only to find empty air because she'd already whirled around and snatched the pouch from beneath my arm and taken off at a dead run back toward the inlet.

I started after her, but angling back to put myself in between the men and her, and prepared to throw myself at both of them if either so much as dared reach for my little sister. I'd been scared before, but this was different; I felt like a bear that had been poked one too many times with a stick and was protecting its cub. At that moment, I didn't care about the pouch or Hamilton or any of it. I just wanted Lillie to get as far away from them as possible.

But Lillie had a whole different idea, and only too late did the men realize what her plan was and started up with a terrific shouting. She ran to the water's edge, drew her arm back, and sent the leather pouch spinning out over the fast-moving water, mail fluttering out like so many white moths before disappearing into the water.

The men passed me by without even glancing in my direction, both of them totally focused on the flying pouch as it hit the water with a loud SPLASH!

"Run, Lillie! RUN!"

But again, she was ahead of me. She reversed course and streaked away from the inlet, Bandit racing beside her with his ears flattened back against his head.

The men ignored them, dived into the water, and reached for the bag.

I followed Lillie as she headed through the coconuts, bound for the thickest part of the jungle on the other side and the towering banyan

tree. She looked over her shoulder at me as she disappeared into the woods, and I looked over my own shoulder to see what was going on in the inlet.

Her throw had been good but not good enough. I saw the short man dragging himself back onto shore, holding the mail pouch above his head. It was streaming water, but I saw it was still half full of envelopes. I couldn't tell if the big envelope from Tallahassee was still in there or not.

But it didn't much matter because they didn't care what became of us any longer. As I followed Lillie into the dark shadows of the forest, I saw the last expression on her face hanging in front of my eyes like a picture. She looked like she was about to cry.

Chapter Fifteen

A Papa's Wisdom

The two men left us alone after they got the pouch with the envelope in it. It burned me to see them gloating and grinning as they headed back up the beach right past our hiding spot.

"No reason worrying about it anymore," Lillie said once the men had gone for sure and we had emerged from our hiding spot. "What's done is done, I guess."

"I guess so," I agreed, more angry and mad than I had felt in a long time. "I guess we should head home. Nothing else we can do here, and who knows if they're coming back?"

But Lillie didn't move. She was looking at the inlet with tears pooling in her eyes. "What do you think happened to Hamilton, Charlie? We still don't know."

I let loose a huge sigh and shook my head. "I suppose I believe those men didn't hurt him. They maybe tried, but…I think he got away. After that…" I let it trail off because

I didn't want to say the next part out loud. But then I looked at Lillie and saw she was watching me, her eyes wide and shining. "You remember what that crossing was like on the way down? My guess is they moved that boat across the inlet to trap him on the north shore. But Hamilton must have figured out what was going on and had time to hide the pouch before they caught up to him. He got away somehow and…I think he probably tried to swim for it, maybe hoping to get the boat and bring it back over to get the pouch and go on his way. He hadn't lived here long enough to know what the inlet is like when the water is up. And then I guess…I guess he didn't make it. Who knows why. Maybe got hit by log. Maybe he just wasn't a strong swimmer."

The tears spilled from Lillie's eyes as she swept her view down the inlet, past the sandy point, and out into the great Atlantic. I knew she was imagining what it must have been like for Hamilton to be grabbed by that current and taken downstream, then out into the sea.

"C'mon, Lillie," I said, reaching down to take my sister's hand for the first time in years. "Let's go home."

***

The walk home seemed to happen in a daze, and later I could hardly remember any of the miles from that long trip. We made the bottom of the lake that evening and took the small boat we hid for just such a purpose back to the island.

It seemed strange and otherworldly to be coming back home. We had been on longer adventures before, but something felt different this time. Maybe it was Lillie's sadness, which I could see weighing on her like a hundred-pound sack of flour. Or, maybe it was my own growing awareness of the things men will do for money and that sometimes the good guys don't come out on top. Mama and Papa always told us that the world was a fundamentally good place and that people who are honest, who do right by others, and who try their best to live a good life will prosper. How many times had I heard Papa talk about the value of "smart work," which was what he called it when a person looked at all the options and took the path that would benefit the most people. "A rising tide, Charlie," he would say, "will always lift all boats. Whenever you have a chance, you want to be that tide."

But everything felt so unfair—Gleason would get his plans just like he wanted, and our friend was still missing two weeks later. I held out hope he was alive, but I knew the danger and risk out here. It didn't matter that neither of those men actually had pulled the trigger. They were responsible for what happened to him, just as sure as if they had shot him. But I knew for certain that nothing would happen to them, and nothing would happen to Gleason, except he would get richer and more powerful.

I was worried too about Lillie. She had grown more silent, sadder, throughout the walk home, and when we got home, she went to her room and pulled the door shut. Mama followed her in, and I heard her crying hard, her voice hiccupping. I didn't realize how much I missed my lively, smart little sister until I saw her like this, and it made me angry all over again.

That night, I found myself pacing the house just like Papa did when he was upset. Mama was in with Lillie again, and I was feeling cooped up and useless. Finally, I went outside to find Papa, who was working on the last pieces of the cane mill. I saw that Papa and Uncle Will had finished turning the logs into rollers and had even built a winch and gear system to turn the whole works. Papa was using the last of the light and the bright moon to finish building the sluice and spigot that would collect the juice from the crushed sugarcane and feed it into buckets. The big kettle Uncle Will had brought back was sitting not too far away under a makeshift hut they had lashed together from thatch to keep the rain out.

Papa looked up from his work as I approached and sat down on the very same log he had sat on just a few weeks before when the snake bit him.

"Hey, Charlie," he said. "You come out here to give me a hand?"

"Not really," I said.

He grinned at me for a second before it faded. "I didn't think so. How are you feeling?"

I looked at my feet. "Well, not too good, I guess." I looked up at him and was glad it was getting dark so he couldn't see how upset I was. "It just…doesn't seem fair."

Papa set down the tool in his hand and walked over, rubbing his hands clean on his pants. He sat down next to me. "Well no, it doesn't now, does it? How's your sister holding together?"

"Not very well," I said. "She's in with Mama again, still crying."

Papa sighed. "That's why they call it a broken heart, I suppose. It hurts just as bad as breaking a bone, maybe worse."

I stared moodily at the ground.

Papa nodded. "For what it's worth, I think you're probably right about what happened. I talked to Will, and we'll still get up a party and go out looking for him, but…"

"Yeah, I know. If he was going to turn up, he would have by now."

Papa was quiet, then said, "You know, Charlie, I know this is hard to hear, but sometimes there's just no explanation for the way things happen. At least not one you can see. You can make yourself crazy trying to find one."

"But…I feel like there's something else we should be doing."

"Like what?"

"I don't know. Writing letters to the governor? Maybe tell Mr. Flagler what happened. Just something."

"Hmm," Papa said. "I wonder if you're feeling a little guilty."

"Guilty?" I said around a sudden lump in my throat.

He nodded. "Lillie told us…at first you thought Hamilton himself might have been working with Gleason, that maybe he'd stolen the plans."

Hot shame burned in my face, and I didn't say anything.

Papa laid a heavy, callused hand on my shoulder. "It's okay, Charlie. To tell you the honest truth, I had my own doubts."

"You did?"

"Yes, sir, I did. And the only good thing about this whole mess is knowing that I was wrong and that Hamilton was every bit the man your mama and Lillie said he was."

"But that still doesn't change anything," I said.

Papa took a deep breath and puffed it out.

"No, I reckon it doesn't. And I wish there was something I could say to explain all of it, but that's the thing about growing up, Charlie. Sometimes you just have to accept that you don't have all the information, and there's nothing to be done about it except try to keep your own head up, do the right thing, and stay true to what you know in your heart is right and proper."

I nodded morosely, thinking his advice didn't make me feel one bit better.

"And, Charlie," he continued, "you did everything that could be expected of you. Sometimes you just have to trust that, in the long run, things have a way of working themselves out. It can be hard, but if you trust the world is a good place, then lots of times it seems like the world will do its best to live up to that."

"I guess so," I said. "At least I hope so."

Papa smiled. "That's what I like to see," he said. "Sometimes it's enough to just hope. Now come on, let's head inside before we get carried off my mosquitoes."

Chapter Sixteen

The Most Expensive Bathtub

A black cloud seemed to hover over our house for the next few days. Lillie emerged from her room, but she wasn't the same, and I hated the look of sadness that marked her face. Even Bandit seemed to notice and followed her with his nose practically glued to her heel.

But living on a farm in South Florida in the summer meant there wasn't a lot of time for reflection. There was too much work to do—and Papa wasn't going to let me loaf around and feel melancholy for too long.

"Up and at 'em, Charlie," he said just a day or two after we got back. "Today's the big day."

Uncle Will was already waiting outside for us as I rubbed the sleep from my eyes and pulled a suspender strap over my shoulder. "What's going on?" I said.

"I think that cane is just about done," Papa said. "And I know for certain the mill is. I thought we might give the works a test run. Just a small batch, mind you, just a taste."

Lillie and Mama materialized as we all trekked to the cane field and watched Papa cut down a stack of cane stalks with his machete, then strip the leaves off with a few swipes of the blade. The cut ends of the cane immediately started oozing liquid, and I could already taste the sweet brown sugar we'd be cooking up.

There was a festive atmosphere as we gathered to watch Papa feed the fat cane stalks into the mill while Uncle Will and I strained to turn the heavy crank handle. The stalks crackled and snapped as they went in, and only seconds later a thin stream of juice ran down the little sluice work and into the bucket at Uncle Will's feet. Papa let out a little whoop while Uncle Will and I sweated over the wheel. Pretty soon, every last stalk had been run through the mill enough times they were dry as paper. The bucket was very nearly full of sweet, clear sugarcane juice.

Next, Papa lit a fire and heated the kettle up. We poured the juice into the kettle and settled in while the fire grew hotter, and soon the juice began to boil.

I'd never seen cane juice boiled up close before. It started as a clear liquid, but once it got to boiling, it slowly turned first a pale golden color and then deepened toward dark brown. And the smell! I'd never smelled anything as sweet and wonderful as that cane syrup, not even Mama's huckleberry muffins cookin'.

It took longer than I expected to boil down

into a thick brown syrup, and we took turns stirring it with a big wooden paddle. As it got darker, Papa fussed around the kettle, studying it like a crystal ball. "We let this go one minute too long and it'll burn," Papa said nervously. Then a minute later, "Alright, Will, let's get this off the fire."

They swung the kettle off the fire and carefully tilted it on its chain to let the thick syrup ooze out into another tin bucket, which Mama used to fill up quart jars. Papa said if we wanted to make actual sugar, we'd have to crystallize the syrup, but that could wait till next time after we got a taste of this batch first. "Besides," he said, "the syrup alone is worth a pretty penny!"

All day, the jars sat inside the house on the kitchen table in rows, cooling while we peeked in every so often. I'd seen a lot of crops grown, of course, but making something like sugar seemed almost like alchemy to me. Mama must have been excited too, because for supper she whipped up a batch of fresh biscuits, using some of her precious white flour and leavening. Finally, after waiting all day, we gathered around the table with the jar of syrup, a spoon for dipping, and a platter of biscuits. Papa wasted no time dipping out a healthy portion of syrup for his first biscuit, then passed the syrup around.

"Here's to the future," Papa announced, and we all bit into our biscuits at once.

I don't know who made the worst face at that table, but the moment that cane syrup hit my tongue, I felt my mouth pucker and my nose wrinkle. Lillie spit hers out immediately, and Mama made a little sort of gasp and dropped her biscuit on the plate. Papa and Uncle Will chewed their first bites and swallowed them down, then reached for a drink at the same moment.

No one said a thing.

The syrup was so salty it tasted like we were drinking seawater. I don't think anyone could have paid me to take another bite.

We all looked at Papa as he stared at the biscuit in his hand. It was still drooling deep brown cane syrup. As if he was hoping for something different, he dipped his finger in the syrup on his plate and tried it again. I could tell from the sour expression on his face that it was still salty. My papa was not a man who cussed, but he swore a powerful oath.

"Maybe it's not all like that?" Mama offered.

Papa didn't answer. I'd never seen him this angry before. Before he could say anything else, he shoved his plate away, got up from the table and went outside. We let him go without a word.

Uncle Will shook his head.

"What's wrong with it?" I asked. "It's not supposed to be this salty, right?"

"No, it's not supposed to taste salty at all, but we live too close to the ocean," Uncle Will said. "The water table must be too high here. The roots reached down to salt water, I guess. They sucked it up and it ruined the cane."

"So that means…?"

"Well, it means you can't grow good sugarcane on Hypoluxo Island," he said bitterly.

Lillie hadn't said anything but was looking out the front door where Papa had vanished. She jumped up and followed him outside.

Mama got up and silently cleared away the dishes, then began moving the jars of cane syrup out of sight. I was left with Uncle Will at the table.

"I'm sorry," I said.

"Me too, Charlie. Me too."

Lillie and Papa stayed outside until the moon was high in the sky, and when I glanced out to find them, I saw them sitting together on the log and looking up at the stars. Papa had looped one arm around Lillie. I saw him lean over and talk to her, and she buried her face in his sleeve. I could only guess what he was saying to help Lillie get over her broken heart. When they finally did come back in, they looked exhausted, but the worst seemed to have passed.

The next day, Papa and Uncle Will went outside and cut down the whole field, then stacked the cane stalks up to dry for kindling. They next took apart the cane mill, and Papa announced that maybe he could build a table or some chairs from those beautiful mahogany logs.

The kettle was dragged behind the house, where Papa declared we had just bought ourselves "the most expensive outdoor bathtub in South Florida." From that day forward, our outdoor bathtub was the envy of every pioneer settler in the region.

We never tried to grow sugarcane again.

Chapter Seventeen

The Barefoot Mailman

Lying in bed that night, it seemed like tragedy had stacked up on disappointment that summer. First, Papa was almost killed by a rattlesnake, and then the expensive and time-consuming cane experiment was an utter failure, our friend Hamilton was missing and maybe even dead, and that scoundrel Gleason stood to get ever richer and more powerful. To top it all off, I knew if Hamilton didn't show back up, I'd be stuck carrying the mail myself.

I fell into a morose sleep, hoping we'd had our share of ill fortune.

I had strange dreams that night, just fragments and snippets of things that had happened and others that maybe were yet to come. I saw a snake lying in the sun, cut in half by Uncle Will's shotgun, and the inlet where Hamilton had disappeared roaring like the biggest wave that ever fell upon the land. I saw Lillie high up in a coconut tree, looking down at me and yelling words I couldn't hear, and I was alone in the woods and heard the crackling of branches as someone walked toward me—someone I was certain I didn't want to find me. I ran through the woods and found myself on the bright beach. There were sharks surging in the shallows off the shore, their fins slicing clean through the water, and silver bait fish bursting from the water like rain. The sand was washed clean like it had just rained, except for a single set of footprints heading down the beach for as far as I could see, the toes making little dimples where the owner had taken off his shoes.

I woke up in the morning wondering what it all meant, then realized why I was awake in the first place: a commotion down by the dock. I climbed from bed, slid into my clothes, and headed out to see Steve Andrews down on the dock with Papa and Lillie.

Lillie was holding something in her hands, and when I emerged from the house, they all turned to face me. They all wore the same expression: shock.

"What is it?" I said, rushing down the path. "Is everything all right?"

Lillie held out her hand, and I saw it was a large envelope addressed to me with no stamp. It had been opened already.

I took it. "What is this?"

It was Mr. Andrews who answered in his

cultivated accent. "Well, Charlie, I was just telling your pa and sister here. I was heading south from the Orange Grove house, looking for turtle nests, and noted some unusual tracks high up on the dune. They weren't turtle tracks, but I followed them regardless and found a hole dug into the sand. It was fresh. You never know what you'll find buried 'round here, so I dug it up, and…well, go ahead and see for yourself. I found it wrapped in leather."

I opened the envelope, and two things slid out. The first I recognized but couldn't make sense of. It was a map with the official state seal on it. The second was a handwritten letter that looked as if it had been hastily scrawled. It read:

Charlie,

If you're reading this, it means I'm right. I think someone is following me. I think it's them fellows I met with Mr. Gleason. There's two of them, both hired men from up in Georgia. I believe they're after the plans for that railroad. I'm not going to let them have it, not without a fight. But just in case, I'm burying these plans now, and I'll come back for 'em next delivery. If I don't, that means the worst, and I hope someone finds these. It'll be up to you if that happens. You're my second. Don't worry, I'll leave a decoy for them to find so you won't be in danger. Just make sure they arrive safely.

Your friend,
Hamilton

I read the letter a second time, then looked up in shock at the ring of faces around me. They were concerned—I could see it on their faces. But there was something else too, and it took me a second to figure it out. They were happy. Papa broke into a big grin, followed by Lillie. It was the first real grin I'd seen on her face in days.

"Those plans they got at the inlet were fake!" Lillie said, unable to hold it back. "He tricked 'em. I knew it!"

"That boy was smarter than I gave him credit for," Papa said. "Wish I'd thought of that."

I found myself grinning along too—I'd never been so happy to be wrong before, and it was like a weight lifted from my shoulders that I didn't even know was there. Then I grew more serious.

"What's on your mind?" Lillie asked. "You worried that bag is too heavy?"

It took me a second to realize she was just teasing, and then I grinned at her, happy to see Lillie acting more like her old self again. "Nope," I said, "I'm just hoping for once I can take a trip without my little sister and her raccoon tagging along."

Everyone laughed at that, even Lillie, and when I looked back later, I realized that was the moment I became the Barefoot Mailman.

Who Were the Barefoot Mailmen?

People take mail for granted today, but back in the late 19th century, getting mail in South Florida was a very long and hard process with sometimes unpredictable results. It could take up to two months just to send a letter from Miami north to Palm Beach.

However, as people like the Pierce family moved into South Florida, it became more important to get regular mail service. That's how the Barefoot Mail route was born. These legendary mailmen included Guy and Louis Bradley's father, E.R. Bradley; Charlie Pierce; and James E. Hamilton. They became famous for walking the mail from the Palm Beach area to Miami and back every week.

The route back then was the same one Charlie and Lillie followed. The mail carrier started at Hypoluxo Island or Palm Beach and headed south to the Orange Grove House of Refuge, where he spent the first night. The next day, he would cross the Hillsboro Inlet on a small wooden boat owned by the U.S. Postal

Service, and then walk eighteen miles down the beach to the New River House of Refuge and spend the second night. On the third day, the mailman would cross the New River, walk to the top of Biscayne Bay, cross the beach dune at Baker's Haulover, and sail down to Miami at the south end of the bay. He delivered the mail from the Palm Beach area, picked up new mail from Miami, and spent the night at the Brickell trading post. The tired mail carrier now had to do the whole thing over again, heading north for three days. In all, the round-trip was 136 miles by foot and by boat.

James E. Hamilton, originally from Trigg County, Kentucky, was the most famous Barefoot Mailman. Hamilton started carrying the mail in 1886. His fateful route began on October 10, 1887, when he left from Hypoluxo Island and headed south. He spent the night at the Orange Grove House of Refuge (in modern-day Delray Beach), then headed to the Hillsboro Inlet the next day.

When he arrived at the inlet, he found the boat was on the other shore, probably taken by a stranger who used the boat without permission. Historians believe Hamilton tried to swim across the inlet and either drowned or was attacked by sharks or alligators.

The truth is, no one will ever know. When Hamilton didn't return from his mail route, Stephen Andrews, keeper of the Orange Grove House of Refuge, and Charlie retraced Hamilton's steps and found his clothes and the mail sack hanging in a tree on the north side of the Hillsboro Inlet. Charlie later wrote in his diary that the river was swollen from recent rains and there were "hundreds of alligators" around the inlet. But to this day, Hamilton's disappearance remains one of the great mysteries of Florida's history.

After Hamilton's disappearance , Charlie Pierce and Andrew Garnett took over the mail route. The Barefoot Mail route lasted until 1892, when an interior trail was cut through the jungle from Lantana to Lemon City, allowing the mail to be delivered by mule and wagon in two days instead of three days. This rendered the Barefoot Mail route obsolete, and it became one small part of Florida's rich history. Much later, in 1937, a bronze tablet was laid at the Hillsboro Inlet, honoring James E. Hamilton, who lost his life in the line of duty. The plaque reads:

THE MAIL MUST GO.

In Memory of James E. Hamilton, U.S. Mail Carrier who lost his life in the line of duty, October 11, 1887.

Who Was William H. Gleason?

William H. Gleason was one of the more colorful characters in Florida's history. While there was no evidence that Gleason actually tampered with the U.S. Mail, he was very involved in the early mail service and was active in state politics and business. Historians have written about the many schemes and plans Gleason tried in Florida in the late 19th and early 20th centuries.

Gleason was originally from New York and went to Yale University. After graduating, he was active in law, politics, and banking throughout New York and Wisconsin. He moved to Florida in 1866, when his family moved into the old military post on Biscayne Bay called Fort Dallas, where Miami is today.

Almost from the first day he arrived in Florida, Gleason realized he could make a lot of money as a land developer. He wasn't the first person, nor the last, to realize this, but he might have been one of the most interesting. Gleason immediately began planning canal and drainage projects throughout South Florida—and he worked hard to gain as much power as possible. In 1868, only two years after moving to Florida, he became the state's lieutenant governor.

That year, Gleason and his allies in the Florida Legislature tried to remove Governor Harrison Reed from office, and Gleason declared himself governor. When the county sheriff wouldn't allow Gleason into the state capitol building, he moved to a Tallahassee hotel and began issuing orders and signing documents as "Governor William H. Gleason," a title he kept for the rest of life. His time as governor didn't last long; a month later, the Florida Supreme Court removed him from office and declared Reed the rightful governor.

After this episode, Gleason moved back to Miami and, at one time or another, held the following public offices: circuit clerk, county clerk, tax assessor, tax collector, member of the school board, Dade County judge, and member of the Florida House of Representatives.

By most historical accounts, Gleason was determined to hold onto as much power as possible. This led to one of his most famous schemes. In fact, this one would briefly affect the entire nation.

In 1876, elections were held for local offices, as well as for the U.S. President. Gleason was running for the state legislature that year but was worried he didn't have enough votes to win the election—so he took steps to make sure he'd win.

When the election was over, officials soon discovered some of the votes from Miami were missing. It was widely believed that Gleason tampered with the vote to change the outcome of his election.

Unfortunately, these missing votes would have huge consequences on the U.S. presidential election. That year, Rutherford B. Hayes and Samuel Tilden were locked in a close election for the U.S. presidency. Without the votes from Miami, it was impossible to certify the overall vote total from the State of Florida and send the results to Washington, DC. Without all the states' results, including Florida, it was impossible to determine which candidate had won the election. Before long, newspapers in New York City were writing articles about the missing votes from Florida.

As the election crisis drew out, Tilden and Hayes reached a compromise: Rutherford B. Hayes would become the new president in exchange for ending Republican Reconstruction in the South.

Later in his life, Gleason purchased land farther north along the east coast and created the settlement of Eau Gallie, where he tried to start the state's first agricultural college. The college was never built, and instead, the only building on the swampy property was turned into the Hotel Granada. The successful hotel burned down in 1902, the same year that Gleason died. Today, Eau Gallie is part of Melbourne, where the William H. Gleason House is on the U.S. National Register of Historic Places.

About Charlie Pierce

Charles William Pierce was born in Waukegan, Illinois, in 1864 and moved with his parents to Jupiter, Florida, in 1872 at the age of eight when his father was given the job as assistant keeper of the Jupiter Lighthouse. At the time, the geographical area that today comprises Palm Beach County was still part of Dade County (Palm Beach County was not created until 1909) and was inhabited only by Native Americans and escaped former slaves. The only white residents were the keeper and assistant keepers of the Jupiter Lighthouse. The Pierce family homesteaded Hypoluxo Island in 1873. In 1876, Charlie's father served as the first keeper of the Orange Grove House of Refuge, located in modern-day Delray Beach, where the Pierce family housed sailors shipwrecked along the beach. It was here that Charlie's sister, Lillie, was born in August 1876. She was the first white child born between Jupiter and Miami, an area that contains approximately seven million people today. Pierce grew up in the jungle wilderness that was South Florida prior to the arrival of Henry Flagler's Florida East Coast Railroad some two decades later. The Pierces were one of the three families that salvaged the 1878 wreck of the *Providencia*, a Spanish ship carrying twenty thousand coconuts. The Pierces helped plant the coconuts that would later give Palm Beach, West Palm Beach, and Palm Beach County their names. During his long, illustrious life as a pioneer settler of South Florida, Pierce served in many capacities, most notably as one of the legendary Barefoot Mailmen who carried the mail from Palm Beach to Miami and back each week. In all, the Barefoot Mailmen covered 136 miles

Left to right: Margretta M. Pierce; Hannibal D. Pierce; Andrew W. Garnett; James "Ed" Hamilton; Lillie E. Pierce; and Charles W. Pierce at the Pierce family home on Hypoluxo Island, ca 1886. *Photo courtesy of Historical Society of Palm Beach County*

The mailman in this mural titled *The Barefoot Mailman*, by Stevan Dohanos, is said to resemble Charlie Pierce. *Photo courtesy of Historical Society of Palm Beach County*

round-trip in six days, rested on Sunday, and then started anew on Monday, for a total of approximately seven thousand miles per year. They were paid six hundred dollars per year in salary. Pierce served for more than forty years as the postmaster of Boynton Beach, after moving to Boynton Beach in 1895, more than twenty years before the city was first incorporated. His son, Charles, was the first child born in Boynton Beach. Pierce served on the boards of various community organizations, as president of the first bank organized in Boynton Beach, and as master of the first Masonic Lodge. His childhood adventures were accurately recorded, and his writings remain today one of the best first-hand accounts of early exploration in southeast Florida. Pierce was farsighted enough to maintain a daily journal from early childhood until late in his life. These journal entries provide the foundation for his book, *Pioneer Life in Southeast Florida*, which is the most comprehensive account of the pioneer settlement of South Florida and the primary reference for most subsequent books on the region's history. Pierce died in 1939 at age 75 while still serving as the postmaster of Boynton Beach. Pierce Hammock Elementary School in Palm Beach County is named in his honor. In 2009, the State of Florida posthumously named Charles Pierce a "Great Floridian," one of fewer than fifty people in Florida's history granted the title. Florida Governor Charlie Crist performed the induction.

Charles Pierce at his desk, ca 1930. *Photo courtesy of Historical Society of Palm Beach County*

About the Author

Harvey E. Oyer III is a fifth-generation Floridian and is descended from one of the earliest pioneer families in South Florida. He is the great-great-grandson of Captain Hannibal Dillingham Pierce and his wife, Margretta Moore Pierce, who in 1872 became one of the first non-Native American families to settle in southeast Florida. Oyer is the great-grandnephew of Charlie Pierce, the subject of this book. Oyer is an attorney in West Palm Beach, Florida, a Cambridge University-educated archaeologist, and an avid historian. He served for many years as the chairman of the Historical Society of Palm Beach County, currently serves on the board of the Florida Historical Society, has written or contributed to numerous books and articles about Florida history, and was named Florida's Distinguished Author in 2013. Many of the stories contained in this book have been passed down through five generations of his family.

Harvey E. Oyer III

For more information about the author, Harvey E. Oyer III, or Charlie Pierce and his adventures, go to **www.TheAdventuresofCharliePierce.com**. Become a friend of Charlie Pierce on **Facebook.**

Visit The Adventures of Charlie Pierce website at
www.TheAdventuresofCharliePierce.com

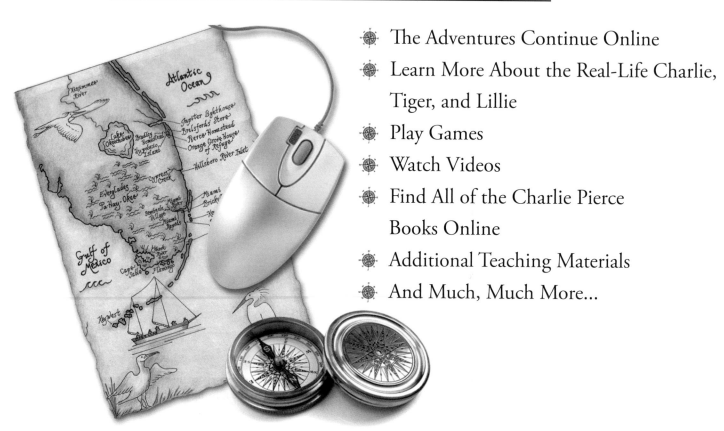

- The Adventures Continue Online
- Learn More About the Real-Life Charlie, Tiger, and Lillie
- Play Games
- Watch Videos
- Find All of the Charlie Pierce Books Online
- Additional Teaching Materials
- And Much, Much More...

The Adventures of Charlie Pierce Collection

The Adventures of Charlie Pierce: The American Jungle
Seminoles, Spanish Treasure & The American Jungle
In 1872, eight-year-old Charlie Pierce arrived with his Mama and Papa in the frontier jungles of South Florida. Charlie's adventures began right away. In this account, based on actual diaries, he explores old battlefields, learns to hunt and boat like a Seminole, faces down hurricanes, and makes an incredible discovery in the sand.

The Adventures of Charlie Pierce: The Last Egret
America's Greatest Environmental Adventure Story for Children
In the late nineteenth century, hunters killed millions of birds in the Florida Everglades to supply the booming trade in bird feathers for ladies' fashion. As teenagers, Charlie Pierce and his friends traveled deep into the unexplored Florida Everglades to hunt plume birds for their feathers. They never imagined the challenges they would encounter, what they would learn about themselves, and how they would contribute to American history.

The Adventures of Charlie Pierce: The Last Calusa
Discover What Lies Hidden in America's Secret River
When famous scientist Dr. George Livingston shows up in the steamy jungles of Florida, he makes teenage Charlie Pierce a very generous offer. He'll pay Charlie $5 a day to guide him and his young assistant deep into the Everglades in search of the rare ghost orchid. But it doesn't take long before the expedition discovers that the swamp is hiding much more than a rare flower as the oldest legends suddenly spring to life.

The Adventures of Charlie Pierce: The Barefoot Mailman
The Mail Must Go!
Charlie Pierce isn't looking for an adventure when he agrees to help out his friend and neighbor Ed Hamilton. Hamilton's job is to walk the U.S. Mail from Palm Beach to Miami and back every week, following a dangerous route that cuts through the jungle and across the water. When Hamilton goes missing, it's up to Charlie and his sister, Lillie, to retrace Hamilton's steps and find out what happened to the missing Barefoot Mailman.

Awards for The Adventures of Charlie Pierce

Florida Publishers Association
Gold Medal - Children's Fiction (*The American Jungle*, 2010)
Gold Medal - Florida Children's Book (*The American Jungle*, 2010)
Gold Medal - Children's Fiction (*The Last Egret*, 2011)
Silver Medal - Florida Children's Book (*The Last Egret*, 2011)
Gold Medal - Florida Children's Book (*The Last Calusa*, 2013)
Silver Medal - Children's Fiction (*The Last Calusa*, 2013)

James J. Horgan Award (Florida Historical Society)
(*The Last Egret*, 2011)
(*The Last Calusa*, 2013)

Florida Book Award
Bronze Medal - Children's Literature (*The Last Egret*, 2010)

Mom's Choice Awards
Silver Medal (*The Last Egret*, 2010)